I0757534

KINSMAN AVENUE PUBLISHING, INC.
www.kinsmanquarterly.org

Black Butterfly: Voices of the African Diaspora

Cover Design by Anastasia Simone

Senior Editor & Design: Monique Franz
Co-Editors: Sandhya Barlaas, Radiyah Nouman, Sophia O. Ofuokwu, and Victoria Sosa

Contributing authors: (top winners) Noelle Kristina Barnes, Y Kendall, Hailey M. Young, and E. Doyle-Gillespie

(in ABC order by first name) Aanika Pfister, Albert Christer Singletary, Alayna Powell, Andrés Amitai Wilson, Anesha Grant, Ava Tiye Kinsey, Blessing Odunyemi, Carlo Kim, Celeste Haehnel, Christopher Neal, Christian Curet, Cianga, Eaton Jackson, Elaine Joy Edaya Degale, Elina Kumra, Jamella Chesney, Jamil Anuva, Kandle Jones, Matthew E. Henry, Michael Eshetu, Michelle Oxford, Monic Ductan, Monique Franz, Mos-X-Tee, Mystery Post, Najib Abbi, Nicole Doyley, Nick Bucciarelli, Norm Mattox, Paula Williamson, Raven S. Wilkerson, Sonia Kinyua, Sufiya Abdur-Rahman, Willy Lizárraga, & Zenobia Anderson.

Black Butterfly

Voices of the African Diaspora

Edited by

Monique Franz

Black butterfly, sailed across the waters.
Tell your sons and daughters
what the struggle brings.

Barry Mann & Cynthia Weil

Editor's Note

When we jumpstarted the second annual competition for the African Diaspora Award, author Nicole Doyley posted the 1984 hit Black Butterfly by Deniece Williams—a song about the survival, faith, dreams, and migration of Afrodescendants. While the nostalgic melody stirred memories of my troubled adolescence and middle school years, I knew instantly that the title was the perfect expression for the upcoming anthology.

This collection marks Kinsman Quarterly's second book of voices from the African Diaspora. Unlike its predecessor, Black Diaspora, a large percentage of the finalist voices were not from the African continent but from the United States. Our review team had no way of predicting who would submit or who would rise to the top, but it became clear that this sequel would reflect our journey post-Middle Passage: surviving slavery, embracing liberation, and continuing the fight for equality and identity.

The poetry and prose from the finalists are arranged around the journey of a butterfly. The section titled Cocoon centers readers on themes of home, family, and heritage. Metamorphosis speaks to empowering transformation from trauma and abuse. Migration captures our struggle with displacement, immigration, and belonging. And finally, Pollination honors the seeds of Black struggle that have blossomed into love, invention, and art that has touched the world.

This anthology is not just a celebration of creativity; it is a map of becoming. As we trace the arc from survival to song, may we remember that every flutter of the Black butterfly is a testament to our strength as Afrodescendants and our power to overcome.

– Monique Franz, Senior Editor

I

COCOON
The Gift and Grief of Heritage

II

METAMORPHOSIS
When Wounds Become Wings

III

MIGRATION
The Restless Flight Toward Belonging

IV

POLLINATION
The War and Bloom of Seeds Sown

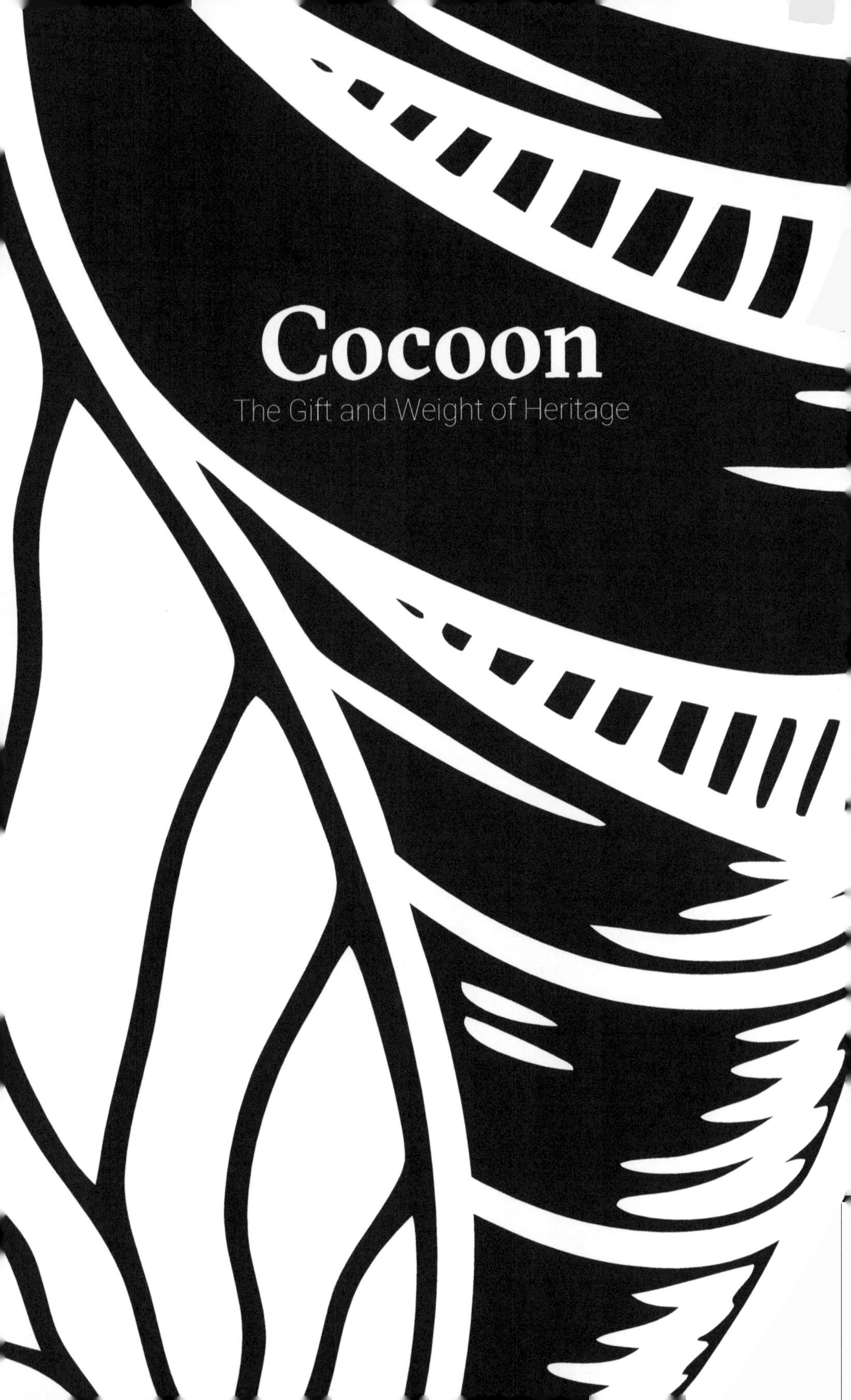
Cocoon
The Gift and Weight of Heritage

Mississippi Mudlark

Mystery Post

Mystery Post

The river brought the girl's body to Nina bright and early that morning. It wasn't the first it'd carried into her path. Nor was it the first she'd haul, heavy and bloated, out of the shallows and onto shore, turning it over so its fish-chewed sockets could gape at the Missouri sky. In her long years of mudlarking the Mississippi river shoreline and shallows, Nina Davis had seen it all. Yellow bones eroding out of the soil on the bank. Stripped naked figures without heads or hands. The freshly dead, calm-faced, looking almost as if they'd fallen asleep and let the current carry them away. She knew right away this one was different.

Judging by the slender form, stiff with rigor mortis, and waterlogged as she was, Nina could tell the dead girl had been young and probably pretty—once. Young and attractive and dressed for dancing.

Her dress was trendy, all lace and satin, with fringe and beading clicking together with each lap of the river's tongue, glittering in the wet light of dawn. That was how Nina had spotted her. On her way to the usual spot, Nina stopped to slip into her waders, seeing the gleam of the dress in the water before she saw the body attached to it. The corpse floated face down, red hair fanned from her head like algae blooming against the gray-brown water. Not the flotsam Nina had been looking for, but the river liked its surprises every now and again.

Suicides and murdered drifters were the most common find and were usually, if not always, men. Not that finding women was rare in and of itself. Murderous menfolk weren't too picky about where they dumped the bodies of their nagging wives, troublesome mistresses, or rebellious sisters or daughters. No, it was the pale skin on this one that set her apart.

White menfolk killed their women just as much, if not more, than black and brown ones, but those bodies rarely wound up here—in the bend closest to the colored part of town. This body was trouble, a trouble Nina felt deeply tempted to let float on by as the limp figure bobbed in the current.

Nina's family lived on the banks of the Mississippi River on the colored side of New Madrid, Missouri, since before the end of the Civil War. They'd been cotton farmers, once by force, then by choice. Next, they were fishermen, then domestics in the big houses on the white side of town. Her aunt still worked in those big houses, watching after the children and doing laundry.

It was a decent enough living for a colored woman in 1920s Missouri, but Nina never had the temperament for domestic work. The river had called to her young, a magic to it that she could not explain but could taste, could feel, rushing in her blood. A magic that did not sit still.

Called to the water, Nina took first to fishing as her daddy before her. But the needs of the river had changed since her daddy's time, and so Nina's purpose changed as well. The decades of settlement, the Civil War and before that, the countless other conflicts, migrations, and moments of historical collidings buried an untold amount of scrap and refuse in the Mississippi silt. The river preferred not to hang onto the trash, but Nina found that some of it could fetch a fair price at the scrap yards if nowhere else. Mudlarking was a hard but honest living. On good days, it could even be lucrative. Not to mention it gave her an excuse to be near the water.

Magic was still okay for folks on the fringes, for poor Black fisherman's daughters with Mississippi River in their veins, folks who knew how to keep a secret. But society at large deemed such old power a thing of the past. And while no one hung witches anymore, no one wanted them around either. A mudlarker, though, could work the banks and shallows of the river in search of what amounted to buried treasure or, at least, other people's buried trash.

This and the surrounding half mile were Nina's turf. Everyone on the colored side of town knew her spot. The other mudlarks respected it and her; left both alone. Whatever she found along this half mile was hers to sell, and any *body* that turned up was hers to deal with or ignore.

Mystery Post

If left, the dead girl would float downriver. Nina could walk away. Maybe go to the south bank instead, pick up digging in the spot she'd started last week. She likely wouldn't find any worthwhile scrap, but she'd avoid the trouble a dead white girl's body could bring her living brown one.

But Nina was old enough to know ignoring the body wouldn't do her any good. Her family had magic and the river and trouble in their blood, and not one drop of hers thought the dead girl floated into her life by chance alone. Nothing, as her aunt would say, happened to their family without reason, especially near the river.

The river put this dead white girl in her path, and now she had to deal with it. Besides, such a fine dress as that had to have cost good money. There had to be someone wondering where it was, where *she* was; someone offering a handsome reward for information, even. Decided, Nina set about pulling the corpse ashore.

She probed first with her pole hook, knocking away the white river crawfish clinging to the dead girl's collarbone. Then, she hooked her under one arm and dragged her close. When she was near enough to grab, Nina inched into the water until it crested her ankles and took hold of the girl's stiffened limbs, pulling her carefully over the rocks onto the bank.

The corpse was heavy, but no more so than any net full of crawdads or lost anchor dredged up for scrap, and that was more the water weight than anything. Soaking wet, the dead girl weighed little more than a hundred stones. Dry, she probably weighed less. The body sank into the red mud parallel to the water, beginning to crack and dry in the rising sun.

It wasn't until Nina turned her to face the sky that she spotted the bruises. A ring of them draped her neck with a matching black-and-blue bracelet on each wrist, another blossomed high on her pale left cheekbone.

Someone had taken hands to her before she died. Nina couldn't say for sure whether she went into the water unwillingly or whether she had all the reason she needed to drown. What she could say was the dead girl had no purse or clutch of any kind. She'd lost her dancing shoes. Mud coated the bottom of her dainty white socks. Nina even checked her collar, hoping for a maker's stitch or a name written by a concerned mother, but there was nothing—just loose twigs and leaves and that all-too-familiar smell.

The girl hadn't been in the water long. If Nina had to guess, she'd say not more than a day. Just long enough to bloat in the arms and legs. Just long enough that the stench of death on her skin was sweet and slick instead of sticky and thick. She was lucky. Most floaters came out of the water black, rank, and stretched beyond human.

If Nina could find her people, the girl would still look herself enough for an open casket. If Nina could find them, that was, and if they cared to have her back. There was only one way to know for sure. Straightening, Nina glanced around, making sure she was alone on this stretch of muddy bankside.

This was the middle of her territory, with no other mudlarker around for miles. She was alone with a corpse, free to do what was needed, unpleasant as it was. Setting her pole hook to one side, Nina prepared for the ritual.

Neither Nina nor her aunt was sure which end of their muddied ancestry passed this strange power down. Nina's mother had had it, and her mother before her, and so on and so on. A gift of blood, an heirloom. It was Nina's now, along with any trouble that came with it. It wasn't a trouble she invited often. Most of the dead she'd found before were people who knew the river, lived their lives by its ebbs and flows, whose spirits already knew how to follow the current wherever it was meant to take them.

Beyond that, Nina rarely saw a need to advertise the skill or paint a target on her back, but this was one of those rare occasions where asking the dead was safer than asking the living. Sure, she could report the body to the police or ask questions around town if there was any word of a missing white girl. But both options were as likely to get her a beating and a night in a cell as they were to get the girl home. Nina had no wish to go hungry or to become some wealthy family's scapegoat.

She'd do her best to give the girl's spirit a chance for rest, but as far as Nina was concerned, her best had nothing to do with sacrificing her safety or livelihood. A bit of blood, though, *that* she could spare.

Nina carefully arranged the corpse's arms, crossing them over her chest, a hand to each shoulder. She smoothed the tangled red hair back from the girl's pale, dead face and placed a flat river stone over each empty eye socket. Only then did Nina take off her waders and step one of her own bare feet into the cool, still shallows, keeping the other firmly planted in the wet, red mud on the bank.

Standing there, at the dead girl's feet, facing downriver, the sun warm against her root-brown skin, Nina could feel the pull of the water on her right heel and the throb of it moving through the earth in her left, the river's lifeblood pounding, rushing past and into and through her. Earth squelched between Nina's left toes. The scales of a largemouth bass, drawn by the body's tempting rot, flashed as it startled away from her.

The Mississippi was alive and well, as it had been since before Nina's great-grandfather had been brought across the sea in chains, when her great-grandmother's Chickasaw ancestors fished the river's depths, when its name had been something else, something far older.

The power of that history built on Nina's tongue, a taste like wet iron filling her mouth as she dipped her fingertips into the water, then the mud. She dabbed her cheeks with the makeshift paint before wiping her hands on her trousers and tightening the kerchief tied around her thickly coiled hair.

As a last step, Nina unsheathed her fishing knife and sliced the pad of her left thumb in the same spot she always did, the white star of a scar marking the point where the knife always cut deepest. She squeezed, and a thick drop of blood welled up out of the wound. Nina let it fall into the red mud next to her left foot; she smeared the next drop on each of the two stones over the girl's eyes and finally fed the third to the rushing river at her right.

There'd been words for this ritual once, incantations spoken in an old language her tongue would never taste, but that part of her inheritance was long lost. The blood, the stone, the water, and the earth were all she had left.

Still, it had never felt quite right to say nothing and just expect the magic to work. It felt dangerous even to let that kind of power loose without something to focus it. So, Nina had taken to addressing the river directly, even if it was only in plain, ugly English.

"You put this one in my path for a reason," Nina said, the burr of her voice soft against the backdrop of the burbling water. "Your reasons are your own, as my will is mine. If it's peace you seek, I'll do my best to put her to rest. But I can't do that without answers." The air seemed to still as she spoke, a sudden, inexplicable quiet building. Even the bugs in the trees, the wind, were silent. The river was listening. Nina took a deep breath. "Your blood is mine and mine I give free. Return her soul for answers three."

Nothing happened for a moment. Nina took it as the river thinking, considering her words or perhaps deciphering them. It was hard to tell.

Then the current surged around her left ankle, a chill lick like the brush of a catfish's mouth, the shock of it sending gooseflesh down her arms and the back of her neck. Nina had a sudden sense that the shallows where she half stood had suddenly deepened, like if she stepped her left foot off land, she'd vanish into the depths without a whisper.

The current lashed the shore and jostled the dead girl's limbs, curving her limp spine as it pushed against her. The first shiver could've been the water or a trick of the light: a shadow passing over the sun, a breeze stirring the branches overhead, tired eyes making out something rested ones would know wasn't real. But the second shiver, the head-to-toe tremble as the dead girl stirred, twitched, uncrossed her folded arms—that was no trick.

Mystery Post

Nina watched warily as the body jerked like a marionette untangling its strings before gaining confidence in its own limbs. In moments, the dead girl was sitting upright, river stones over her eyes falling away as she pulled in a ragged, wet breath through water-clogged lungs and coughed, hands fluttering up toward her chest as she struggled to pull in air with organs not fit to pump it.

"What..." The dead girl's first word was rough and gurgled, a choked-up bit of river weed falling from her lips. Even Nina couldn't help but wince at the sound, but the girl persevered. *"What happened?"*

"You died," Nina said flatly, knowing there wasn't time to waste softening the blow.

The dead girl lifted her head, examining Nina sightlessly. For a moment, the corpse's features blurred in the haze rising in the humid air, and Nina saw a flicker of her face as it must've looked in life: fiery green eyes and full lips, high cheekbones and soft ripples of red hair. Then the image was gone, another trick of the light.

"I... fell," the corpse said after a moment of collecting her thoughts. Her voice was clearer now, an accent to it foreign to Nina. Irish maybe? *"No... he pushed me."*

"Who pushed you?"

The girl took another shuddering, unnecessary breath. *"Daniel Morgan."*

Nina couldn't help rocking back on her heels at the name. The Morgans were one of the richest, most powerful families in Missouri. They kept a big, fancy summer house in New Madrid, where her aunt worked cleaning sometimes. Daniel was the youngest son, the baby of the family.

Nina had to bite her tongue to keep from asking again, just to be sure. There was no purpose wasting a question, hoping for a better answer than what she'd already been given. Not when she only had two left. Not noticing Nina's reaction or not caring, the dead girl continued.

"We drove out to the bridge," she said. *"To look at the sky. He kissed me sweet, like always. Then he had his hands 'round my neck. I scratched him and he grabbed my wrists. We fought and he let me go and I ran. I lost my shoe, and he came running up behind... and... he pushed me. Into the water. Couldn't swim. I never learned. Couldn't breathe. It was dark and cold and there was no up or down."*

"He killed you." It wasn't a question, just a statement of fact, but the girl nodded, the movement jerky and strange. There was something wrong with her neck.

Nina could've asked why. But why ask when she could guess?

Maybe the girl was someone he'd kept on the side, and he'd found someone else, or his family had found out about her and wanted it cleaned up before the news got out, or maybe she'd angered him somehow and the rage had bubbled over. Or maybe he hadn't needed a reason at all. It didn't matter, not really.

Nothing could justify what he'd done, but being rich and white and a man with power was usually enough for the world to forgive any sin. Knowing the why wouldn't help Nina or the girl any. Not unless there was a way to prove it, or the girl had friends or family powerful enough to make him pay for it.

"You got family?" Nina kept her voice steady. She could hear the pain and fear in the girl's voice, but she had to stay focused on the task at hand. Had to watch how she phrased things. The magic winding around them both was tangible but fragile, slippery. Nina had to fight to keep hold of it, as if she were dragging a net against the river's flooded current. She was already sweating with the effort.

"No." The girl shook her head. *"Some cousins back in Ireland, but my parents have been dead for years. I was staying with a friend in Jacksonville, but she won't want me back. There's no money to send me home for burial, and all I did was cause her trouble."* A hesitation. *"She warned me about Daniel. I didn't listen."*

Friends forget the past a lot more easily when there's no future," Nina said. "I can let her know you're gone, at least. See if she can get you buried up Jacksonville way."

Even as she said the words, Nina cringed, thinking of the difficulty of getting a body all the way to Jacksonville, the questions the friend would ask, the danger still presented by the Morgan family if they were to find out their dead girl had been found and had been talking to the living.

"*No*," the girl repeated. "*I don't want to drag her into my mess. But you… you can help me.*"

Nina's spine stiffened, her shoulders drawing back. "I've given all the help I can," she said. "It's time for you to rest now. If you don't have a home or kin to miss you, I can bury you here. It'll be peaceful, it'll be—"

"*It'll be you covering up Daniel's crime for him.*" The girl's sightless sockets were now locked on Nina's eyes, a flicker of something strange glimmering in their darkness. "*He doesn't deserve your help more than I do. He can't get away with what he did to me.*"

"I'm not in the business of solving crimes or dishing out revenge," Nina said. "If you want to waste your afterlife haunting him, go ahead. But I can't help you with it."

"*Yes, you can,*" the girl insisted, the flicker growing brighter, her body straightening and lurching as she got to her feet. "*You have to. Please.*"

"I don't, and I can't." Nina stood her ground even as the corpse lurched toward her. Though a few hands taller than Nina, the girl was whip-thin, as if a stiff breeze might carry her away. "Think, girl. If he murdered you, I don't imagine your sweetheart would have any issue doing the same to me. And then there wouldn't be anyone left to pull my spirit out of the drink afterwards. Ain't no kin of mine left with the gift but me. There'd be no one to trouble him at all."

"*Why pull me out of the water if not to help me?*" The girl trembled as another chill breeze tossed the leaves of the trees overhead. "*Or *were you only hoping to get something out of it? If I was some rich debutante with family money, would you help me then?"*

"I pulled you out 'cause the river wanted me to." Nina crossed her arms. "'Cause the water don't know you and didn't know how to claim you. I offered to get you back to your people. Asking any more of me is your greed, not mine."

But Nina felt greedy. She wouldn't say so, not aloud, but yes, greed was why she was saying no. Greed for life, greed for peace. But so what? So, what if she had pulled the dead body out of the water in want of greed? So, what if she'd hoped that fine dress would lead to a fine reward? In this life, you had to take what you could, survive however you could. It wasn't fair, not for either of them, but that was the world. Nina was too greedy to risk her neck for someone already dead and gone, and the dead girl had no right to judge her for it. "I'm sorry for your troubles, but they aren't mine. I won't pay for them."

Unable to argue with Nina's point, the girl turned away, gazing at the trees and bankside around them, her shoulders curving downward. *"I grew up next to a river back home,"* she said after a moment. *"It was beautiful there, too. And hard and hungry. And poor. I left chasing something better. Now, no one will ever know what happened to me. And Daniel, he'll just get to keep on living, like my life was nothing."*

Nina's expression softened. "He'll get his in time," she said. "I know it may not seem like it now, but he will. Nothing God likes to punish more than pride, and that boy and his family have more than their fair share of sins to spare beyond that."

"That's not enough."

Nina shrugged. "It's all you have."

Breathing out a final, ragged sigh, the girl nodded. The motion was still jerky, and the grace and fire she'd found moments ago were already fading, the magic winding down. One more question and her soul would be gone, though either way, Nina didn't think she'd be able to hold the magic for much longer than a few more minutes. She could already feel the strain—a soreness in her legs, a tightness in her chest, a burning in her arms. Soon as she let go, the river would whisk the girl's soul away again.

Folding carefully back to the ground, movement heavy and slow, the girl lay on her back, fingers brushing over the fine beading of her dress before she crossed her arms, shoulder to shoulder again. As she did, Nina once again saw a flicker of some strange light deep in her sockets.

"He's done this before, you know?"

Nina flinched, toes gripping the earth as her feet slid in the silt. She'd been about to ask her last question, about to get the girl's name and then send her spirit back to the river, but the words died in her throat, another question jumping to her lips instead.

"Done what before?"

"There was a girl before me, a maid from his father's house. He told me about her once. Told me she drowned." Her voice grew softer. *"There was a girl before me. There'll be another one soon."*

Then she was gone. Nina felt the magic break. The stillness in the air shattered like thin ice. The sound and the heat of the coming day rushed back in all at once, hitting Nina like a punch in the gut. She sat down hard in the wet mud, suddenly breathless, gasping like a fish left to flounder on the rocky shore. The magic had taken its dues and then some.

Nina felt drained and tired and hot and sore. Like she'd been working a full shift at the docks. Empty, like she hadn't slept or eaten in days. Almost as empty as the corpse still lying on the bank in front of her. Still nameless. Hollow sockets still gaping skyward.

She should bury her, Nina knew. Before the bugs came and the smell got worse, and the rotting started. If she wanted to keep her greedy peace, if she didn't want word getting back to the Morgans about a dead white girl washing up on the colored side of town, Nina should bury her. But all she could think of was the dead girl's last words: *There was a girl before, there'll be another soon.*

Nina remembered hearing about the death of a maid who'd worked in the Morgans' house in New Madrid. A pretty, young, black girl who'd hit her head on the dock behind the house and drowned in the river not two months after her sixteenth birthday. Her momma and daddy went to Nina's aunt's church.

When the praying hadn't brought them peace, they'd asked Nina to summon their daughter's soul, but the river didn't hang onto spirits that long. Especially not the ones it knew. There'd been no calling her back at that point. No goodbyes, no answers. Just the pain of not knowing what you didn't know.

It should've made Nina feel some type of way that she cared more knowing Daniel Morgan had murdered more than just the one poor, pretty white girl, that he'd murdered a colored one too. It certainly made her a bad Christian, but to be fair, Nina had never claimed to be a good one. She *had* felt for the nameless dead white girl sharing her riverbank. She'd just felt for her own safety more. Against one death, her life had felt more important. But against two, soon to be three? That was a harder sum.

"Shit." Dipping her cupped hands into the Mississippi, Nina splashed water onto her face, cooling herself down and catching her breath. She could still walk away. She could bury the body and the trouble with it. Move on with her day, on with her life, leave the bones for the mudlarker after her to uncover and wonder over. But the river had put this in her path for a reason. And burying trouble was no better than trying to run from it.

When she felt stronger, Nina stood up and walked around the corpse, so she was standing at the girl's head rather than at her feet. Remembering the spark of something bright and awful and righteous in the dead girl's eye sockets, Nina remembered the Black girl's parents. How little comfort she'd been able to offer them. How little justice. And there came her anger. Stronger than fear, stronger than greed, bursting its banks, overwhelming good sense.

Who was she to dish out revenge? Who was she to make a white man pay? Well, who was Daniel Morgan to take what he wanted with no thought to cost? Nina kneeled, washing the dead girl's hair before picking up the blood-stained river stones that had fallen and tossing them into the center of the river. This time Nina would leave the corpse's eye sockets open. She got up, stretching her aching back, wiping sweat from her brow. She had work to do.

This time, Nina stepped her left foot into the shallows and planted her right in the cracked Mississippi mud. The wet iron taste of the river filled her mouth again, stronger than before. She dipped her fingers into the water and the silt, and dabbed her forehead and upper lip, and scraped her hands through her hair, pulling it down loose around her shoulders.

Unsheathing her knife again, Nina sliced the pad of her opposite thumb, the one on her right hand. This magic would require more than a few drops of blood, though. Daniel Morgan had already spilled more than that. Blood for blood. That was always the first and highest price.

Flicking her knife clean, Nina pricked the tops of all her fingers next, right and left, and then cut across each palm. The blood welled, the pain snaking through her body like a current. Nina crouched down, pressing one bleeding hand into the mud by her right foot and plunging the palm of the other into the water at her left before lifting both and gripping either side of the corpse's face with wet, muddied, bloodied palms.

"One more time, Ole Miss," Nina said. "I offered peace, now I offer blood. Give me your fury and your flood."

The river darkened, a harsh wind whipped the trees, the blood from Nina's hands pooled in the hard angles of the dead girl's face, and once again, the body stirred, coming back to life with a deep gasp. A hard, cold, dark red light flickered to life in the otherwise empty sockets and fixed on Nina's face.

"Welcome back," Nina said. "What do you say we pay a little visit to Daniel Morgan?"

Shuddering, limbs twitching, the dead girl smiled.

A Feminist
Interpretation
of the Massacre

(poetry collection)

E. Doyle-Gillespie

E. Doyle-Gillespie

A Feminist Interpretation of the Massacre

With a frantic swirling of your hands,
you take up your hair
like a Gibson girl,
then look at me with
the sudden clarity of sleep.
Standing on the edge of the bed,
wearing a concert T-shirt
that we've shared between us
down to a faded rag,
wearing the panties that ride
higher on one hip than the other,
you tell me your vision of the Zong.
They must have made a charm bracelet
of the African women, you explain,
standing on the edge of my bed.
Chained at the ankles,
each to the next,
on the 29th of November,
with the ship's water running low,
you say that the Dutch gentlemen
must have ushered those ladies
to the open window
with the utmost of care.

Deciphering the Ghosts of Your Haunted House Novel

Do they haunt this house
because it once owned them?
These ghosts that you wrote?
Is that what we are to read and glean
from each chapter-passage?
That when you wrote the nameless *haint*
who drifts up and down
the grand spiral stair,
you were saying that she'd
been manacled there?
That the oldest one was bound
to the house by the cast-iron heat
of an ancient stove?
That "The Silhouette Boy" in the garden
was the shade of a gambling bet
collected by the master one day,
two-days' carriage ride away?
And did you mean that
in the mansion's middle passage,
over a sea of over 100 years,
from plantation to wedding venue celebrations,
their names had gained manumission
and only their engram shades remained?

E. Doyle-Gillespie

Mojito Conjuring

When the bruja in the red dress
sends me out this time,
it is for the taste of
sour oranges and garlic.
Once, when I plied her
with a cigar called Hoyo de Monterrey ,
she coiled the smoke,
said that I was still feral and untamed,
sent me out for sugar so that
I could learn my name.
Scythe-swinging, field-slave-singing,
I could not return to her coven of one
until I had learned that my "Suarez"
meant that I was the son of sugar itself—
the child of wild ingenious devouring
the rows of cane like a dragon.
Now, red-dress bruja breathes out
clouds of tobacco negro,
turns the cigar round and round,
tells me to gather garlic and aurantium oranges
so that the sour and the sucre may jibe
together in me,
and leave me properly christened
for when it is time for me to work,
time for me to sing,
time for me to sweat.

Pepper, in Those Days

He pauses at that
point in the story,
each time, and makes
a shaking gesture
with the palsied right hand.
Sharp bones
jut up against
his thin brown wrapping
as he feels for the next
set of words.
It is a motion like gathering
and then sprinkling—
spreading out pieces
and scattering grains.
It is a motion
like struggling against
something hidden.
This is when he tells me
about how the women put
pepper in their shoes,
and ran the brown boys down
to wait in the swamp.
Black pepper would throw
the dogs from their scent.
Then, they could
wait for the passing of the hounds,
and the anger,
and the set jaws
of white-sheeted men
who tied such perfect knots.

E. Doyle-Gillespie

The Busker's Candomble

Actually, I take that back.
I take that back as far
as I can take it back—
as far as I must—
without it fading me to black,
without it turning me
to dust that you blow
into the face of an unwilling horse
of your goofer dressage.
I take that back:
She does still wear the black hat—
that top hat bergère-style.
When she takes her cello
and takes her walk down to the
metro stop, to the taxi stand,
she wears the black hat
with that rakish tilt
of Papa Legba.
It still has its peacock feather with
its glowing blue eye.
It still has its ring of skulls,
its ring of bones,
but her father's candomblé has
gone cold beneath its brim.
Her candles' wax is frozen
in the shape of its last melting
on her mantle,

and her salt waits in jars
to make circles on the kitchen floor.
Her candomblé has gone desuetude,
and she lays that hat on sidewalk
top side down.
She takes a bow,
takes up her bow,
waits by the gate,
and the hat overflows
as she plays Ring of Fire
and the multitudes throw
their shekels in the rush-hour dusk.

Burning
or a Bullet

Noelle Kristina Barnes

Noelle Kristina Barnes

You couldn't pay me to swim in Starke Lake. Long before I was murdered there, I knew of feet that lost toes to piranhas in those waters, mothers who lost children because they underestimated Starke's depths. As many times as I may have imagined losing my own children, even I couldn't stomach the idea of leaving them unattended anywhere near that lake.

But where Central Floridian families lost legacies, pit vipers found mates. A scorned Lucy Rankin, at the end of her rope, witnessed their passionate orgy during a tearful midnight stroll. Unfortunately for me, the spectacle of dozens of snakes recklessly splashing their sex near Starke's shoreline somehow salved Lucy's pummeled heart. Inspired, she stared, storing the memory of pit viper mating season in that dark corner of her mind where the devil held court.

In the fall of 1920, the last drops of October rain under the third quarter moon announced the arrival of pit viper mating season alongside the beginning of harvest season for our Hamlin oranges. Eva Mae was ten, Henry Jr. was eight, and Willie was sixteen months old. My time was mostly spent sewing buttons back onto the work shirts my husband tore working in the citrus grove, stitching up holes in the children's clothes, switching Willie from hip to hip, canning, salting, and cooking. My nights were largely spent campaigning for a refrigerator and counting down the 1,455 days left before Willie could join his siblings at the schoolhouse.

Daydreaming of freedom was my second favorite pastime. Daydreaming of Clarence Rankin was my first. For over a year, Clarence and I would steal a few minutes away together here, and an hour or so there. After Willie turned fourteen months, we snuck away for an overnight trip. Henry Sr. didn't mind me taking the train alone to "check on a sick cousin" as long as I had someone lined up to tend to the children while he worked. Clarence was a painter, so

I bribed my landscape-loving hairdresser with a new addition to her art collection if she'd be my stand-in.

We took four trains to get to Manhattan Beach in Jacksonville. A drink from the Fountain of Youth in St. Augustine was planned for spring. Clarence inhaled imagination and exhaled adventure. Creativity oozed from his pores and mixed in with his paints to create colors I didn't expect to see until I got to heaven.

It's no wonder Lucy Rankin was out for my blood. You might be too if I borrowed your husband as often as I did hers. But if you ask me, evil's been brewing in her spirit long before I came along. I couldn't understand why Clarence stayed around.

"Lucy can't have no kids, and Clarence don't want none," Pearl informed me the last Saturday morning in October while hot combing my hair at her kitchen stove. "There's not a pot too crooked that a lid won't fit."

Pearl Carter knew everyone's secrets. For one, she was a little on the short side. Women tend to confide in ladies under five feet in ways they don't confide in taller women like myself. But Pearl also deserved credit for just being a good listener. I must have been an even better one though, 'cause her lips were always loose around me.

"MOMMA! H.J. hit me!" My daughter's shrill scream came from the front yard. Pearl laid her hot comb on the stove so I could get up.

"Stop yellin', Eva!" I whispered as loud as I could out the window. "Your lil' brotha is tryin' to sleep." I peered over at Willie on the sofa in the sitting room. Thank God he stirred only slightly. "HJ! Quit bein' ugly," I continued. "If I have to come out there, that tree you hidin' behind can't save you!" My mind lingered on Lucy's luck. Can't have kids? What must she be doing with all that freedom?

Pearl continued as I settled back into my chair. "Lucy and I spoke after that meetin' our Women's Ministry had with Mary

Bethune a few weeks ago. 'Member I tried to getcha to go to that meetin'?"

"Naw, I don't recall that, Pearl." I remembered alright. I was on cloud nine after my cousin Henrietta told me she'd watch the children that day. I thrust my hand into my left pocket. Clarence's latest invitation was still there.

"Did ya know her husband was a painter?" Pearl asked. I detected accusation in her voice.

"Is that a fact?"

"Shole is. Met him this Sunday past. Lucy invited me and Carl over for lunch after church."

My ears pricked up. Pearl Carter knew everyone's secrets, but she couldn't know mine. Could she?

"I convinced Carl to buy one of Clarence's paintings. You know I loves me a good landscape." Pearl leaned over to catch my reaction before returning her focus to the next section of hair.

Pearl and her husband, Carl, owned fifty acres of land in Ocoee and ran a turpentine distillery. The Carters also owned a refrigerator, a car, and a few properties they rented out. I hoped Clarence got some good money for his work, but I began to sweat a little.

Pearl pointed to the far-left wall in her sitting room. Silver and purple shimmered on the surface of a peaceful river, while the setting sun flaunted a pretty little palette of pink and lavender in the sky. The view through the pine trees framing her new canvas reminded me of someplace Clarence and I had probably made love. Hanging in the hallway outside Pearl's bathroom was the painting I had given her. Framed in gold, a white ibis preened underneath a stately palm tree on a deserted beach.

"You picked the perfect spot to display it, Pearl. It's a beauty." I changed the subject. "I hear the sheriff let Mizzus Milton out."

Pearl shook her head. "It's about damn time. Cryin' shame how they treated her."

All the old woman wanted to do was register to vote. It was the first time women had been allowed to in her lifetime. Meanwhile, the only reason my name is on the Orange County voter rolls is on account of losing trick after trick against Pearl playing Pinochle the night before she'd planned to register. I lost a bet and was forced to join her and four other ladies from the women's ministry on their trip to the voter registration tent. That Saturday in September was more humiliating than I could have imagined.

We were each required to write our full name, birthdate, age, and address on the voting certificate. They sent Genie Edwards home when she forgot you spell Ocoee with two Es instead of one. Told her, "Orange County voters must know how to read and spell."

We watched them turn Mamie Colston away after she "illegally" attempted to register as a member of the Democratic Party. Lily Roundtree was shown the door because she didn't have the $2 to pay her poll tax. The sheriff threatened to arrest Pearl when she offered to pay for her. Poor old Mizzus Milton. They did her the worst.

"What's yer full name, gal?" We all cringed at the white registrar's disrespectful tone after she'd handed him her certificate, but Mizzus Milton didn't bat an eye.

"Mizzus Lula Daisy Milton," the widow replied.

"Lula Daisy..." the man scoffed. Disgust scrunched his face and then narrowed his eyes; her certificate was incomplete.

"And just how old are you, Mizzus Milton?"

"I'm 67."

"Is that right? Well, what year were you born, gal?"

At this, Mizzus Milton froze. Her slim shoulders slumped. Then, the old woman lifted her head towards the sky. I imagined she was praying for the good Lord to sneak into her head the memory of a math lesson she was never taught. All of us there who'd been blessed with the lesson ached to give her some assistance, but we'd seen what happened to Ms. Junie after she offered old man Pritchett similar sympathies; banned from the registration tent for life, the sheriff said.

Mizzus Milton's silent seconds seemed to stretch on for hours before a surprise olive branch was extended her way.

"If yer 67," the registrar offered, "that means you were born in 1850, right?" Mizzus Milton seemed to want the ordeal over and done with. "Yes, I reckon I was." She paid her poll tax and hobbled away from the registration tent looking triumphant.

She didn't get far before the sheriff approached her with handcuffs; a warrant had been sworn against her for perjury.

Meanwhile, in one of the four whites-only registration lines, I spotted Miss Tessie. The disheveled daughter of a drunken farmhand knee-deep in gambling debts didn't have the money to pay her $2 poll tax, nor any shoes to cover her feet for that matter, but she had blonde hair and green eyes; assets enough for the supervisor to let her register anyway as a "one-time courtesy."

If it wasn't for practicing the registration with Pearl, who learned everything from Ms. Mary McLeod Bethune's workshops, I would've probably left that tent in handcuffs myself. Related troubles ran across my mind as Pearl lay her hot comb on the stove to get more hair grease.

"How Carl been doing since his accident, Pearl?"

"Chile, that wasn't nobody accident. Them dirty crackas was followin' Carl since he left Orlando! I thought being run off the road might sit that man down somewhere, Dee, but he still refuses to take a hint. When Carl got his mind set, all I can do is hope the Lawd stay tuned into my prayers."

"I heard Carl bragging to anyone who'll listen that his missus a registered voter now."

"You think my vote enough for Carl? No. Dis fool have to plot and plan to get every Negro in town to the polls! That white Republican lawyer in Orlando got 'em all riled up."

"The enemy of my enemy is my friend, what they say…" I offered.

"You right, Dee, but when white friends help…"

Pearl shook her head as she gently guided the comb, sizzling and crackling as it made contact with the grease. "Lotta times the help turn into the hurt. Where was the Republican when the Democrat tried to run over my husband?" She parted another small section of my hair. "I'm glad Clarence agreed to help 'em."

"Clarence helping Carl get folks to the polls?" My mind ran in a million different directions.

"Long as Lucy give him permission to take her car, bless his heart," Pearl giggled. "Imagine that, givin' your husband permission to drive your car."

Didn't Carl have all the help he needed from the Knights of Pythias? I thought. *For Christ's sake, why was he dragging Clarence into their fight? I wondered if Clarence would've been so helpful if Carl hadn't bought that painting. Damn, Pearl and her highfalutin' landscape obsessions—*

"Ouch!"

"I'm so sorry, Dee, hold your ear down, please."

I did as instructed, wincing from the burn. My coils surrendered to the heat, but I saw a window, so I played it cool.

"Pearl, you think you could watch the kids for a couple more hours before dinner? I'm fixin' to drop off some soup to Henrietta in the Southern Quarters. Poor thang got a nasty fever after this mosquito bite—"

Pearl slammed her hot comb down on the stove and came around to face me. I could smell what must have been an expensive perfume.

"Delphine Bulah Collins, I have tried my very best to be a good friend to you. But I'm not as blind as your ol' man. You can't expect me to just sit by like I don't know from nothing. How I'm s'posed to look Lucy in her eyes, aiding and abetting your affair like I am?" Finally, she was out with it.

"Pearl, I God! You think I'm havin' an affair? Why in the world would you think that?" Pearl grabbed me by the wrist, yanking me up from my seat with a force I didn't expect from her small frame. Once in the hallway, she pointed to the bottom right corner of the painting which hung outside her bathroom.

"Take a good look at that signature."

I peered and squinted, but my show did not go on for long before my wrist was again yanked behind me, and I was dragged to the sitting room. We stopped in front of the newest addition to Pearl's art collection.

"Now, look at this signature, Delphine. Tell me Clarence ain't paint this one and that one you gave me months ago when you went overnight lookin' after Henrietta."

"OK, Pearl, yes, your paintings might be by the same artist, but that don't mean I'm lettin' the artist cut a slice!"

"But thennnn—you miss da Woman's Ministry meetin'. And Clarence happen to be alone 'cause Lucy at that same meetin'."

"Pearl, you know I had to watch the kids. Henry was fertilizing the grove. He don't like how I act after them meetings anyway—"

"Umm hm. You right about that, Dee. That's why I ain't think nothin' on it. Now here you go askin' me bout watchin' the chi'ren today, and you know what today happens to be?"

"It's just any ol' Saturday, P—"

"Says you! It's choir practice day at the First African Methodist Church."

"And what does that have to do with me?"

"Lucy sing in the choir at the First African Methodist Church, Delphine. She gon' be away from home for hours this afternoon. And I betchu her husband gon' be gone too!"

Willie Jr. stirred again at the sound of Pearl's raised voice. I rushed over to softly stroke his eyebrow, a trick my mother taught me.

"Stop it, Pearl Carter, just hush yo' mouth! OK, you found me out. And I'm mighty shamed for what I did."

As Willie settled back into dreamland, I plopped myself down on Pearl's chaise lounge. "I didn't tell you 'cause I rather die 'fore anyone know 'bout my sin. I know it don't matter one bit Henry slacking in his husbandly duties and treat me like his fourth child most of the time. That's my cross to bear, and Lucy shouldn't be paying that price."

Pearl nodded her head in agreement. "Everybody got a justification for sin these days," she sighed.

"You right, Pearl. And I been prayin' about this long and hard. That's why I'm endin' thangs today. I just need you to watch the chi'ren this last time."

Pearl rolled her eyes and twisted her mouth in disbelief.

"Aw come on now, Pearl. What?"

"Soon as you see Clarence puppy dog eyes, you'll be beggin' for your next left-handed honeymoon!"

I could understand Pearl's fears, but she could never understand what life was like for a woman like me. My husband was too broke for paintings and perfumes, and he was too stressed to be charming. When he proposed underneath the camphor tree in my momma's and daddy's front yard, he gave me a bigger diamond than my grandmother's Missus wore (let my momma tell it). He convinced me my beauty burned bright enough to light his passion for a thousand years, and that it would warm the world up to the both of us. Life as the wife of a citrus grower was sweet for some time, but a few years after Eva Mae was born, some white men from Orlando started coming around. Then, rumors began spreading that Henry's citrus grove was infested with pests. We lost buyers, and Henry was forced to drive down the price of his oranges. More men came around questioning the legitimacy of Henry's property deed. Can you imagine selling your diamond ring just to hire some lawyer to prove what's yours is actually yours? After that, the anonymous threats started. Henry didn't let me read the letters, but the fear now living in his eyes told me all I needed to know.

"Your husband seem to thrive off the fight. Injuries and all. But Henry? Fighting that never-ending war to keep our citrus grove… it's stolen all the spark from my husband's spirit. I love my husband, and I didn't cheat on him for lack of self-control, Pearl. I did it out of starving for some light."

Pearl shook her head again, but when she looked back up at me, her eyes softened. "The road to hell was paved with good intentions, Delphine. Now, go head on back in that chair so I can finish straight'nin' you out."

***

Later that Saturday afternoon, I watched Clarence from my seat on the worn blanket covering the mossy ground, our spot underneath a cabbage palm on the shore of Starke Lake. He was naked, arms akimbo. I was scared shitless he was going to get himself hurt; if I had to choose between Black people voting and him staying alive, my people might never see the inside of a voting booth a day in their lives.

"So, what I'm s'posed to do, Dee?" Clarence's eyes widened as he searched mine for answers I wished I had. His sculpture-perfect penis flailed a bit, punctuating his confusion. "Knocking these crackas out only leads to niggas strung up in a tree. Ducking these crackas and sneaking around like a hunted criminal ain't no kinda life either. Mr. Leecher swear he'll have me arrested for quitting his potato fields. But I can earn better wages in the citrus groves. Locked up, Dee! For trying to make a better living?"

He shook his head, grabbed his pants, and began to get dressed. "The man who drive us to the groves gotta pay $2,500 just to get the license he need to stay outta jail hisself. These old-time slavery laws ain't going away 'til we vote the devils out who support them!"

32

"All this time, Carl and his Knights been getting voters registered just fine without you," I continued. "Now, all-of-a-sudden, they don't have the manpower to take these same voters to the polls?"

"Dee, everyone got their role to play in all this. All them Knights, you right. But only one or two have cars. Tuesday is important. All us need to be down there."

I jumped at the sight of a dark figure and the sound of leaves crunching in the distance. Probably just a deer, but I was visibly on edge. Clarence strode towards me and grabbed both my hands; his touch was gentle but firm. He spoke softly.

"You scared them white folks got somethin' planned?"

I shook my head before wringing my hands free. I turned my back to him and lied to the pine trees.

"Ain't nobody 'fraid of no silly ass crackas. I just don't see the point is all—voting." I turned back to face him. "The whole thang about who can lie well enough to convince fools life gon' change once a man like him get behind a big wood desk that my great-great-granddaddy carved, inside a big white house that your great-great-uncles probably built."

Clarence furrowed his brow. I grabbed his ears and kissed that brow, eager to drop the matter. "Can I come with you to Tampa next weekend when you go sell your paintings?"

He stiffened a bit. "I already promised Lucy, Dee."

I blinked hard and swallowed my tantrum, kissing his lips and twirling my tongue around his. "I thought it was supposed to be my turn?"

"I know, baby, but Lucy would butter my bread and then slice my throat with the same knife. 'I'll cut you in your sleep if you don't take me!'" he mocked, in what I imagined to be his wife's raspy, biting tone.

I narrowed my eyes, angry that my kiss couldn't bend him to my will. Grabbing my blanket from the ground, I folded it with haste. Clarence pulled me back to him and spun me around to face his longing.

"How about we make a deal, little lady."

***

"Momma, Ms. Greene say class ending early on Tuesday so she can go vote."

Here we go with this again. It was only Monday, and already Ms. Greene was sending my child home stirring up trouble.

"Ok, baby, thanks for letting me know." I turned back to the greens simmering on the stove.

"Are you voting on Tuesday, momma?"

"No, chile."

"Why? 'Cause the white folks don't want us to?"

***

Tuesday morning's sky was gray, filled with clouds waiting to release their loads. Henry and his workers prepped bags, ladders, and clippers to start picking the Hamlins, and my eldest children were off at the schoolhouse. I calmed my nerves with a shot of moonshine instead of cream in my coffee and slipped well-worn-in Louis heels on my feet. With Willie strapped into his stroller, I set out to tackle a new responsibility.

When we finally got inside the polling tent, I opened my handbag and felt inside the fabric enclosure to find my voter registration certificate. It was still there, just as it was two hours ago when I first secured my place in line. I straightened out the pleats in my skirt and wiped the sweat from my face. They found any and every reason to turn us away. Looking disheveled was bound to fit one of these white inspectors' criteria for showing me to the exit.

"They said we'd neglect our children when we got the vote," came a young woman's voice. I looked over and did a double take.

Standing directly across from me in the line reserved for whites was a clean-faced, hair-coiffed Miss Tessie. Her filthy overalls had been swapped for a respectable skirt, and she even wore matching heels.

"They was wrong," she continued. "We bring 'em with us."

She held her five-year-old son's hand while she smiled at Willie and me. Those nearest Miss Tessie in line watched her, appalled at with whom she'd chosen to strike up a conversation. "Yes, ma'am," I smiled back, picking Willie up to wave hello as more heads turned. "Train up a child in the way he should go."

I finally approached the polling clerk. To my surprise, I saw another recognizable face. "Well, I declare! Mizzus Collins?" Mr. Benjamin Harold looked down his cheaters, then quickly toward the door behind me.

"Good mornin', Mr. Harold. Didn't expect to find you sitting behind that desk."

"Didn't expect to find you in front of it." His eyes darted behind me again as if he was urgently expecting someone else. The last I saw of him, Henry had given Mr. Harold a steal of a deal on a bushel of navel oranges the man planned to ship up north. I wasn't too keen on Mr. Harold: it was strong-arming that secured him that deal.

"Yer husband know you came down here?"

"Why wouldn't he?" was my quick reply. I smiled wide to smooth over my sass.

"Let's getchu in-an-out, Mizzus Collins. You don't wanna be lingerin' round here. Lotta folks don't want ya'll anywhere near this place. I couldn't look yer husband in the eye if somethin' were to happen to you."

"I don' intend to linger. Just tell me what you need from me so I can make my vote. Here go my registration."

"To yer right, second row center, there's an empty booth. There's a pen you can use in the booth, but make sure you put it back now, or the next voter won't have one."

"I have my own pen, so—"

"And you have your own husband too."

I'd never heard her speak, but the raspy rage in her voice struck a familiar chord. "Leave mine alone, or I'll cut ya every way but loose."

I dropped my pen and turned around to face one of the prettiest women I'd ever seen. Chocolate skin without a mark. Hourglass figure. Almond-shaped eyes. She was almost my height, but I relished looking down at her, nonetheless.

"You must have me mistaken, Auntie. I don't know your husband from Adam." I whipped my head back around to face Mr. Harold.

"Oh, you know my husband sure as I know the devil," she hissed, grabbing my left shoulder to twist me back around. Lucy shot a glance at Mr. Harold to make sure he too was listening before she turned back to face me. "I'm not gonna tell you again. Leave Clarence alone or leave this earth."

She narrowed her eyes and gave me a final once-over before striding haughtily towards the clerk at the next table. I suddenly felt smaller than a flea as she unclasped her leather handbag to retrieve her certificate. I looked around that polling tent and felt all the confidence I'd practiced seep out of my pores like sweat. I looked for Clarence under that tent, but he was nowhere to be found. Instead, I found Miss Tessie's eyes, and everyone else's, on me like white on rice. The inspectors snickered, victorious without having to lift a finger. Too embarrassed to stay, I turned around to leave.

"Mizzus Collins!" Mr. Harold's voice stopped me in my tracks. "Your pen."

I slowly about-faced and stepped cautiously towards him. My head lowered: I reached out for the pen. It was placed in my hand along with a ballot. I looked up.

"The Klan marched round here on Saturday," Mr. Harold recounted. "I know they ran Mr. Carl off the road last week. None of that mattered, and you came down here anyway. Now, some jealous woman lyin' on yer virtue got you all set to turn back and run home with yer tail between yer legs?"

I grabbed the ballot from Mr. Harold before Willie and I made our way over to an empty voting booth closest to the exit just in case a quick escape was required.

***

I made it back home, put Willie down for a nap, and started fixing dinner. A quick choke on his rooster would be both Henry's dessert and his lullaby, but after I'd gotten the children fed and into bed hours later, Henry still hadn't made it back to the house. This was typical if the packing house had a big shipment to prepare for up North, and the timing couldn't be more perfect. I could put Eva Mae in charge and have a legitimate excuse for leaving the house: searching for my husband. I tucked Bessie in my left pocket since it was near sundown and locked the door behind me.

I thought briefly of bloody, buttered bread as I walked down to our meeting spot near Starke Lake. Would Clarence even be there after what happened at the polls? He promised me that if I worked up the nerve to go cast my vote, he'd take me down to the jook joint near the tracks in Lakeville.

Had I been in my right mind, I might have smelled the smoke, turned my gaze up Orange Avenue, and spotted the flames rising from the First African Methodist Church. But my thoughts were locked down on Clarence and the run-in with Lucy. I only came back to earth on account of a sudden wave of water that drenched my feet at the shoreline.

"You shole is built like a mule. Always ready for a ride, huh?"

I jumped at the unexpected sound of her raspy voice and turned around to face a wild-eyed Lucy Rankin careening toward me in the dark. I dodged swiftly to my left, reached into my pocket, and pulled out Bessie. Lucy leaped backward as I swiped my 9-inch blade in the air. Then, from the same leather handbag I'd admired earlier that day, she pulled out a revolver.

"What is it? Huh?" she tossed out, as I put my hands up in surrender, never dropping the knife. "What you got that man think I don't have?"

Funny enough, I'd often wondered the same thing. Without kids to tie him down, why couldn't he just leave Lucy? What kind of spell had she spun? I'd pondered, plotted, and spent so much time picking me and her apart, I wasn't thinking about what needed thought.

A frenzy of splashing sounds intensified behind me.

"I told you earlier to leave Clarence alone or leave this earth," Lucy continued. "You made your choice. You thought you were meeting him here tonight. But he ain't coming for you. Now, I'm going to give you another choice. I can shoot you in that pretty face of yours, or you can cool off in the lake."

I didn't want to take my eyes off her, but I knew something bad was happening in the lake of which I should make myself aware. I slowly turned towards the water and couldn't believe what I saw: dozens of slithering serpents entangled, thrashing about on the surface of the water.

"What you look so scared for, Delphine? They's yo' own. How can a snake be afraid to swim with snakes?" Her laughter was throaty—maniacal.

I'd like to tell you I was able to reason my way out of that last meeting with Lucy. I'd also like to tell you I was right in figuring the snakes might have more sympathy for my misplaced passions than she did. But I can't. What I can tell you is if I'd stayed home that violent fall night, I would have faced similar choices: burning or a bullet. Same as Henry and our beautiful children. Same as Pearl and

Carl. Much like dozens of other Black people in Ocoee who hadn't already fled the desperate mob of broken white men hiding behind soiled sheets and sullied crosses; men above the law who'd grown tired of the impotence of their lies, threats, and intimidation. If I could go back and make different choices, I'd spend less time trying to steal what was Lucy's and more time fighting to hold on to what was ours.

Leaving Gillespie's Pointe

Monic Ductan

Monic Ductan

Two houses stood on the south beach of our island, built by the family of Raymond Gillespie—the man for whom our island was named. They stood side by side, twin daughters—one white, one brown—both perched on stilts, gazing out at the ocean. The white daughter wore a turret tower, cocked like a hat atop her head. The other, as tall and regal as her sister, was painted brown and had a red door that, to me, looked like a streak of blood running down her belly.

We all knew that Raymond Gillespie's family had spent their summers in the houses going all the way back to the early 20th century. And then, for reasons unknown, the Gillespies stopped summering on Gillespie's Pointe. I had no memory of the family at all—only the speculations people shared about where they might have gone. Some said they'd switched to Tybee Island, St. Simons, or some other place that promised more than our island's quiet, half-deserted beaches and the hope of full fishing nets.

For as long as I could remember, the two houses stood vacant. But the summer I was seventeen, my cousin Victoria and I saw a white girl in the yard of the brown house. We had been sitting on my cousin's back porch, the wire grass swaying to one side in the breeze. The brown house rose behind the girl, perched on its stilts, its windows winking in the sunlight.

"Who is that?" Victoria asked.

I opened my mouth to answer but shut it quickly. The wind gusted bits of sand into our faces. I squinted at Vic through the grainy dirt, eyes watering.

"Think we should go talk to her, Lena?" Vic asked. Strands of her black hair whipped across her face.

Everyone always said Vic and I looked alike—and I guess we did. Same dark skin. Same top-heavy mouth. Large, dark eyes that slanted up at the corners.

My eyes teared to push out the dirt, and once the wind settled, I wiped them with the back of my hand.

The girl began waving her arms back and forth.

"Well, she's looking over this way," I said, "like she wants to get our attention."

Just as we started down the beach toward her, a voice called out.

"Where y'all going?"

I groaned before I could even see the boy the voice belonged to: The Ugly One.

I had two cousins—twins. One had a gnarled, deep scar from his cheek to his chin. He was the one who kept his hair in ropey dreads, and because he didn't use his psoriasis cream, he had white patches of flaky skin on his face, neck, arms, and even his back. His brother, who kept his hair shaved like peach fuzz and lathered on the cream, was better-looking. That's how they got their names: The Good-Looking One and The Ugly One. They stayed on the south beach behind Vic's house and cast their nets on weekends.

The Ugly One blocked our path. He often ridiculed me for being dark-skinned, even though he was the same shade—maybe darker.

"Don't start on us," Vic warned.

The Ugly One usually treated Vic a little better than he treated me, probably because she'd once bloodied his nose.

Vic kept walking toward the girl, her long legs leaving me behind. I admired her posture and height. I was much shorter, with a large chest and a round bottom.

"I ain't scared of you!" the Ugly One yelled, making a big show of walking backward in front of us.

Once we reached the edge of the beach, Vic and I left the twins behind and climbed the embankment leading to the brown house. Though I'd lived on Gillespie's Pointe my whole life, I had never set foot in this yard. Granny and the old folks made it clear—we were not to trespass on the Gillespie houses.

Up close, I could see the brown house's chipped, peeling paint, and the porch sagged a little in the middle. Vic's house, built shotgun-style, sat to the right of my clapboard home. From up here, our houses looked so small.

The twins cut through Miss Mason's backyard on their way back to their trailer, their long, lean bodies disappearing into the sagging moss of a willow tree. Meanwhile, the girl on the hill moved cautiously toward Vic and me.

She greeted us in a low voice. "I'm Jilly."

Jilly had taken too much sun—her red face and peeling arms testified to it. She was thin to the bone, her knees and elbows poking through her skin.

Vic stepped forward. "You Mr. William Gillespie's grand-girl?" she asked. William was descended from the original Gillespie who'd owned the rice plantation. We didn't know much about them—except that they were rich.

"William Gillespie is my great uncle. My daddy's uncle. My mama was a Bingham."

"Don't know any Binghams 'round here," Vic said.

"We're from Alabama," Jilly said. "Birmin'ham. But we're going to live here now."

"You mean—you're summering here?" Vic asked.

"No, we're registering me for school and everything."

Vic and I looked at one another. Summer people were only supposed to be summer people. We hadn't heard anything about a new family moving in. Our island had fewer than 100 residents, and all of us were African American and descendants of slaves. I was related to everyone on the island in some way or another.

"Y'all go to East Bay High?" Jilly asked.

Vic nodded. "We're seniors this year."

"I'm going into the eleventh grade." She sighed and looked at the ground. "I don't have any friends yet." She looked as though she might cry. I hoped she wouldn't.

A second later, she smiled and invited us in. We nodded, but I could feel Vic's nervous energy as we followed Jilly toward the back of the house.

To see inside a Gillespie house felt like a rare treat. We stepped into a kitchen, and to my surprise, there was no air conditioner humming, not even a window unit. The air felt stale. In one corner, the linoleum peeled up from the floor, and a brown stain covered a big patch of the ceiling. The old-fashioned gas stove had eyes that needed de-greasing, and newspaper was draped over the kitchen table instead of a tablecloth. The paper had once been wet and then dried—I imagined someone peeling wet shellfish there, crabs or shrimp that caused the newsprint to run together.

Vic picked up an overflowing laundry basket with a pair of men's underwear draped over the side. She set it down on the floor to clear space at the table. I took a spot beside her. The chair I sat in was tall and straight-backed with uneven legs—I imagined it had once been beautiful. When I scooted back on the seat, my feet didn't touch the floor.

My cousin and I exchanged looks. Where was their expensive fridge that made ice on the outside? Their beautiful paintings and silver tea set?

Jilly walked through a doorway and into a dark room. The boards creaked under her feet as she moved.

When Jilly came back into the kitchen, she had a bandage on her finger and carried a box fan. She set the fan down on the floor and plugged it in so that warm air blew across my leg.

"Travis came to my porch last night," Jilly said. She looked back and forth between us.

At first, I didn't know who Jilly meant, but then Vic asked, "How do you know The Ugly One?" and I remembered that Travis was his real name.

Jilly was silent for a moment, obviously confused by the hateful nickname, and then she asked, "How'd he get that scar on his face?"

"Got into it one time with a guy who cut him up good," Vic said.

A disgusted look came across Jilly's face as she uttered the word *horrible* and shook her head. Jilly opened the fridge and took out three small bottles of apple juice, which she shared with us.

"Travis wants me to go down to the beach and meet him tonight," Jilly said.

"Girl, don't go," I said.

Vic followed with, "Stay 'way from him."

"My daddy would kill me if he knew I was going with a Black—" she paused. "It's just that—"

Vic interrupted her. "My mama and daddy would kill me if I brought a white boy home."

Jilly let out a relieved breath. She skirted the table and sat down across from Vic and me. The newspaper rustled as she scooted her chair to the table.

"The Ugly One," she said, then corrected herself by calling him Travis. "He wouldn't be so bad-looking if he cut that hair of his," Jilly continued. I didn't dare look at Vic to see what I knew would be a disgusted look on her face, lest I crack up.

Vic swallowed with a big gulp, then said, "He to' up."

Jilly shook her head. "How's he torn up?"

Vic set her juice down on the newspaper and started to tick off a list on her fingers. "His skin, his scar, his hair—"

"I don't mind the scar," Jilly said. "It makes him look dangerous, kinda sexy."

This time I did look at Vic, struggling to swallow. The juice gurgled around in my mouth, its acidic taste stinging my throat.

***

A few weeks later, Vic and I sat out on my front porch. There was a smidge of daylight left, and the evening air was cool. I pulled the sleeves of my old sweater down over my hands and hugged myself. An engine rumbled, and I looked up and saw a white Ford pickup with a gun rack in the back window. The truck pulled up on the grass right alongside the porch railing. One front tire rolled over Granny's white lily. Granny would have a fit, but she wasn't home just then.

"I'm Charlie Gillespie," a white man said to us through his truck window. I wondered if he knew his truck wheel was on our flower. "I'm looking for my daughter Jilly. She in the house there?" he asked, nodding toward the door.

"No, she ain't," Vic said. "You checked with her boyfriend?"

Charlie Gillespie's brow knitted together. "She don't have one," he said.

"Sure about that?"

Gillespie's face flushed red.

"Vic," I whispered.

Gillespie cut the engine and poked his head out the window so far his shoulder nearly cleared the windowsill. "Who is he? He live around here?"

"We don't want her to get in trouble. You should ask her yourself," I said.

Charlie Gillespie got out of the truck and came up to the top porch step. Vic and I looked up at him from where we sat.

I heard laughter out at Karen's place, a few houses down. I looked around Gillespie's hip to see Granny leave a pack of older women in Karen's yard. She started down the hill, heading across the field toward us, one hand on her hip, her flowered skirt swishing back and forth. I lived with Granny—she'd raised me since my parents left to find work on the mainland.

Just as Gillespie looked over his shoulder to see what I was looking at, Granny stepped into the edge of our yard.

"Who you?" she asked him.

He waited until Granny had walked a few paces closer before answering, "I'm Charlie Gillespie. Looking for my daughter Jillian, a blonde-headed girl," he explained. "She's 'bout this tall," he said, holding his hand up in front of his chest. "She didn't come home today. Thought y'all might've seen her."

Granny shrugged. "Why would you think she over here?"

"My wife told me these girls are her friends."

"Guhls," Granny said, looking at Vic and then at me. "Y'all seen his daughter?"

We shook our heads.

Gillespie stared at Granny. Finally, he said, "When my wife and I came home today, we saw someone had cut down our clothesline and scattered trash all over our front porch." He paused, awaiting a reply from Granny. When Granny didn't answer, the man continued. "That 'un right there," he said, pointing at Vic, "she told me Jillian has a boyfriend, but I don't know anything about it."

"And you think we do?" Granny asked. "It ain't up to us to keep up with yo' guhl." She put her hands on her hips and stared at him. Then, she stepped around him and up onto the porch, positioning herself between the man and me. "I believe my grandkids done tol' you they don't know where she at," she said. "Now back this truck off my flowerbed, Cholly Glispie."

One corner of his mouth lifted in a smirk. He stepped backward down the porch steps, climbed into the pickup, and left.

***

A few nights later, we were on Vic's back porch, listening to the waves, and Vic kept steering the conversation back to Jilly.

"She thinks she's better than us because she's got The Ugly One," she said. It was dark out, so I couldn't see her face, but I could practically hear her rolling her eyes.

The island was full of gossip about the two lovers. After Gillespie left us on the front porch that day, he had a confrontation with Jilly and The Ugly One. Jilly tried to catch the afternoon ferry with him. Gillespie intercepted them and warned The Ugly One to stay away from his daughter.

"Her daddy probably broke them up," I told Vic. "And anyway, why would we care that she's got The Ugly One?

"Because he's Black," Vic said. She sighed, and when she spoke again, she sounded like she was talking to a little kid. "Jilly thinks she's got a leg up on us. She thinks she's won something."

"Won what?" I asked.

"Don't you ever get tired of losing all the time?" Vic sighed. "Losing our men to their women. Men like The Ugly One will jump over every Black girl to get to a white one." She started to say something else, then paused. "And property taxes. Why do we have to pay all this? Our ancestors made this island what it is, built it on their backs, and now we have to pay whatever the greedy *buckra* wants."

Vic continued her rant about white people. I'd heard it a million times before.

"White people love money!" was one of her favorite exclamations that year. Property taxes on the island had more than tripled in the past few years, and everyone saw it as a push to get rid of us islanders and develop the land into a resort town.

"I just hate what that would do to our home," Vic said.

I pointed out to Vic that she was itching to go to college on the mainland, but she glared at me.

"I wanna leave by choice, not be pushed out! If you don't know any better than that, then you don't know me."

Unlike Vic, I hated confrontations, and I couldn't find the courage to tell her that I didn't like how angry and bitter she'd become. She was my first cousin, my blood. I needed to keep her in my life, so it was just easier to ignore the parts of her I didn't like.

***

Spring came. We graduated. Our island family threw us a big graduation party. Less than a week afterward, Vic caught the mainland ferry and was gone. Not seeing her every day was hard for me, especially in those first few months. She and I talked on the phone each week, but those conversations became fewer and farther between after she started school and I began going to community college and working full-time at a mainland diner.

Granny's health deteriorated. She'd always had high blood pressure, and she had her first stroke not long after Vic left. She wasn't completely immobilized by it, but the stroke slowed her movements and changed her speech.

One evening, Granny lay propped in bed, half a dozen pillows around her. The bedside lamplight illuminated her twisted mouth. The glaucoma in her eyes had turned them a grayish blue. Her entire right side was visibly smaller than her left—the shriveled arm and leg looked useless. She caught me watching her, and I must've had a frightened look, because she said, "God won't put no more on me than what I can bear. Don't worry, chil'. It won't be long."

I began to cry, inaudibly, and leaned over, pressing my face onto her bed. When my nose caught the scent of peppermint on her bedspread, I shook and sobbed. I'd never felt so lonely before or since. That night, I longed to have someone. Anyone. The obvious choice was Vic, but she was in Mississippi—gone. Soon, Granny would go too.

***

Granny began to talk about death all the time in those days. She'd call me into her room, her voice weak and raspy. I'd sit by the bed and listen. She told me I'd have ownership of the house we lived in, and that the house next door would be a family home co-owned by my aunt, my cousins, and me. I was instructed not to sell the land or the houses, which she didn't need to tell me. The importance of keeping the family's land had been ingrained in me since childhood.

"You'll live here in this house with JJ someday, when he's out of the service," Granny often said. She sounded so sure of herself that I almost believed her. JJ was the boy who had grown up on the island with Vic and me. Just as we started to show romantic feelings for each other, he joined the army and was deployed the year before, when Bush invaded Iraq.

Like Vic, JJ had kept in touch with me at first, but slowly his phone calls became fewer. Before he left, I'd imagined Granny alive and well in this house, and that JJ and I would live in the house next door. Vic, of course, would still live in the other next-door house. All three houses lined up in a row. That's what I wanted. Back when I'd made those plans, I had had no thoughts of Vic and JJ leaving me—and no thoughts of Granny dying. They all were permanent fixtures in these houses, on Gillespie's Pointe, and in the world.

I looked at my dying grandmother: I wasn't strong enough to tell her what was in my heart. Somehow, I just knew that JJ wasn't coming home. Wasn't he already making the life he wanted in the military? In all those months away, he'd probably scarcely thought of me.

"You and JJ," Granny said. "And dem big, strong Gullah babies."

Granny had been telling me about Gullah babies all my life. She said we came from strong stock. Our ancestors had survived the Middle Passage, fought and survived through slavery, and then fought harder to keep our home here on the island. She'd always said the Gullahs were strong and should be proud, but I knew she didn't think much of mine and Vic's generation. Afraid we didn't have enough pride in our traditions, she feared we'd leave the island like my mama had.

"There will always be Black people," I said to her once during our last summer together.

"I reckon," she replied. "But da Gullah ways gwine die."

One rainy morning in July, I went into Granny's room to get her up. Usually, I'd prop her in bed or help her into her rocking chair by the window. She liked hot milk with tiny flecks of oatmeal and cinnamon for breakfast. She'd have that or some grits, and I would purée fruit for her. Then, I'd wait for Miss Mason or one of the church ladies to come sit with her while I went to class or to work.

But that rainy July morning when I went into Granny's room, she couldn't be roused. She lay flat on her back. Her chest neither rose nor fell. Her cheek had turned a little cold, the way your toes do when they lie uncovered at night.

I called Miss Mason on the telephone. Within half an hour, the house was full of people. The women gathered around to ask about the funeral arrangements.

***

The next day, someone came to my bedroom door and knocked softly. Figuring it was Miss Mason, I lay facing the wall and didn't even roll over.

"Morning, Miss Mason," I mumbled, then realized I should've said, "Good evening."

"Lena?"

I'd know that voice anywhere—even in a noisy, crowded room. If that voice were to whisper to me, I'd recognize it.

Before I turned over, I felt Vic sit down on the edge of the bed. I rolled over slowly. Vic's mouth fell open when she caught sight of my face. Even without a mirror, I knew my eyes were swollen from crying. I hadn't combed my hair or brushed my teeth either.

She leaned over and hugged me. "What can I do to help you?" she asked.

She wore a navy blue pantsuit and looked grown up. Her black hair had streaks of brown in it and was cut into a neat bob that brushed across her collar when she moved her head. She took off her black pumps and gently nudged me over so she could rest more comfortably on the bed. Vic stretched her long legs out in front of her, laying her shoulder against the headboard.

We'd lost touch, which I regretted. A couple of times I'd even failed to return her phone calls. I'd been so preoccupied with Granny and studying and work that everything else had seemed unimportant.

"I don't think I can go to the funeral," I told her.

She nodded. "I understand, Lena. But what I want to know is, what are you going to do now? Granny's gone."

I sat silently for a moment. "Now, as in, what will I do with my life now?"

She squeezed my hand. "Yes."

My voice broke the silence. "Take me with you. When you leave to go back to Mississippi, take me with you."

***

When we were kids, Vic and I rode around the island on an old two-seater bicycle. A few days after the funeral, we decided to take the two-seater from her father's shed and ride around for old time's sake.

"Let's go to the oak trees," I told her from the rear seat. Though I couldn't see her face, I sensed her rolling her eyes.

My favorite place on the island was one that Vic didn't think much of. It's a sandy dirt road. The trees are huge—some of the tallest on the island—and they're covered in gray Spanish moss. Two gnarled oak trees stood on opposite sides of the roadway. Their branches hung over the middle of the road, the tips of their limbs touching in a high arc, the same way that little kids' fingers touch when they play London Bridge.

The only paved road on the island is Ferry Road, and all the sandy dirt roads branch from it. As soon as we hit the dirt road leading to those oak trees, Vic angled us around a big rut in the middle of the path. She groaned loudly.

"Don't know why you want to come to this old, bushy place. It's so wild."

When we were in middle school, Vic claimed she once saw an alligator crawling out of the marsh and heading toward my favorite oak trees. It scared the hell outta her, and she'd hated this spot even more since then. (We don't see many gators around the island, and when we do, they usually wind up on someone's stovetop.)

Vic came to a stop, and I put my feet on the ground to help balance the bike. Looking up at the tree branches, I sighed. God, I would miss this place. On afternoons like that one, the sun hits the moss and the branches just right, and everything glows. Sun-dappled. That day was breezy, and the wind played in the Spanish moss, waving it back and forth like long, slender banners.

"It *is* kinda pretty," Vic admitted.

We rode up and down the dirt road, going back and forth under the trees, avoiding the ruts and bumps. I closed my eyes under the canopy of trees, enjoying the breeze.

When I was a middle-schooler, I climbed one of these oaks—higher and higher—as high as I could go. Finally, I looked down and was stunned to see the space between my body and the ground. I looked out and saw the tops of the houses in my neighborhood. Some of the roofs were patched. I could see clear out to the ferry dock in one direction and straight out to the ocean in the other.

***

They all came out to the ferry dock to bid us goodbye—Vic's parents, Karen, Lonnie, Miss Mason, the church ladies and deacons, and the Shacklefords. The wound of losing Granny was still fresh, and it was coupled with two new blows: saying goodbye to my island family and leaving my home.

By the time we loaded our suitcases onto the ferry, I was a blubbering mess. I couldn't stop crying until we finished weighing down Vic's car with suitcases at the mainland ferry and were headed down the highway.

I'd never been to Alabama or Mississippi, and I also knew very little about Georgia, our home state. Underneath the sadness and uncertainty, I felt excited. We rode through a never-ending series of small towns before finally making it to Atlanta, the biggest city I'd ever seen. I couldn't get over how many lanes of traffic their interstate had or the number of Black people I saw driving nice cars. *Suburbanites.* They were so different from most of the slow-talking, country Blacks I knew on the island or even the ones I saw in Beaufort.

When we stopped at a hotel outside Birmingham, the clerk, a cute Black man with a wild afro, asked if I was from up north.

"No," I said. "Georgia."

"I'd have guessed New York or someplace," the man said, smiling at me.

The more I read and studied, the less of an accent I had. I kept grinning until Vic said, "Why are you so proud to sound like you're not from home?"

I didn't respond right away. I followed her up to our room and dropped my suitcase down outside our door as she fumbled with the key card.

"What do you care? You left home quick as you could," I said, surprising myself at how bitter I sounded.

She raised her eyes to me from the door's lock. The light flashed green, and I put my hand on top of hers, pressing down the lever that led the way inside the room.

Once we'd settled our things on opposite sides of the queen bed, she finally said, "You resent me for leaving?"

I walked toward the bathroom, deciding to ignore her, but then I whirled on her and said, "Yes. All those nights I was so lonely and scared. I wanted you with me."

"Then why didn't you call? I can't read your mind—"

"You knew she was sick. It wasn't a secret," I said. And then everything else came out: how she was no fun to be around at times, being so eaten up with anger. "And I've suffered too. Gillespie's Pointe is my home as well, and it kills me to see that in another generation or two, it may be a completely different place. Everything's changing, and I can't even talk to you about it."

I went into the bathroom, slammed the door, and sat on the lip of the tub. Fuming, I cried until I thought she'd fallen asleep.

Finally, I went back into the room and lay down beside her. When she turned to face me, I asked, "Did you scatter the trash and cut the clothesline?"

After a pause, she said, "I shouldn't have done that." She rolled over on her back. "Always talk to me—especially when I do or say something wrong."

We lay there in silence for a moment.

"I'm angry about some of the same things you're angry about," I said, "but just being angry won't get us anywhere. Who is there to be angry at anyway? Gillespies? White people?" I groaned. "We have all this pain and nowhere to put it."

"We can put it on each other," she offered. "Talk about it, I mean."

And we did. And we have ever since.

Fourteen Ways of Looking at a Mullato Boy

(poetry collection)

Andrés Amitai Wilson

Andres Amitai Wilson

Fourteen Ways
of Looking at a Mulatto Boy:

1. Mother with brown nipples and black coils
    under checkered quilt, interrogated
    by paternal grandfather–white, flaky head.
    "Are you sure your milk's the right
    color?"

2. "I'm white," the toddler asserted to his maternal grandpa,
    a veteran of WWII and paterfamilias. "But how
    can you be white if your mother is
    Black?"

3. Back-to-School-Night (when they were still
    together), he in steel-toed work boots and flannel,
    she in Ethiopian braids and teacher's skirt,
    ablaze with music notes;
    that night, for the first time, the playground
    called him "zebra."

4. "Nigger, chink, spic—
    I'm not sure what to call
    you." So, he uses them all.

5. Zebra stripes become chameleon colors—the boy
    could act! But the casting agent tells mom, he's
    "precocious," "adorable," and "too
    ethnic for the role."

6.   "I've never met a Black kid as white
     as you," says the white kid
     with the backwards hat and baggy pants
     who spits the N-word
     as if it were
     his.

7.   "I always think of you as my Black friend,"
     says his *best* friend. "But you're just as Irish
     as I am."

8.   Black on the basketball court,
     talkin' shit as best he could in the accent
     he learned from rap CDs,
     but a proper prep school lad with the "Yes, sirs"
     and polite smile to the
     policeman
     at the routine traffic stop.

9.   "Black kids don't skateboard; Black kids don't
     play guitar; Black kids play basketball. Why don't you
     play basketball anymore?" asked the dark cousin
     with the black "X" on her shirt.

10. "But what else are you?" demand the two
     Black girls of cornrows and FUBU who kinda
     look like his mom.

11. At music school, the virtuosic rock guitar audition,
     with all of the distortion and searing leads, lands him
     the gig in the
     all-Black gospel choir.

12.   The Dominican guy at the bodega calls him "Papì"
     and insults his high-school Spanish. "Why you
     parents never teach you Spanish?"

13.   *Isn't race just a social construction,*
     and don't I merely exist in its interstices?
     Nah, bruh. *One drop* makes your choice for you.
     You a house nigger; no slinging cotton,
     but still cleaning pots in da kitchen.

14.   On an admissions form or job application,
     always check "Black,"
     but on a mortgage,
     Don't. Remember, you could be Barack Obama;
     You could be Alicia Keys; you could be
     Colin Powell (isn't he just light-skinned?)

Not Black enough, you'll never be white.
Alas, no one wants a post-racial world anymore,
             no one, that is, except
             for us tragic mulattoes.

DISCO DON

Uncle, you have the bic-bald head
of your father, smooth and shiny, a corruscating
crystal ball of dreams, and I rub it for good
luck and to show I love

You, because men don't say
such things to each other.
Silent, my love for you is, Uncle,
silent like the entire generation you ended.

You burst through in '44, the last
to earn a good wage and be a company
man, until Woodstock burned it all
to moonbeams and cow pastures;
(At least that's the way I imagine it all.)

But you weren't all that Norman Rockwell,
all that Buddy Holly.
First of all, we're black,
and secondly, like your Boomer siblings,
you preferred disco to Dylan,

It's crystal as shiny as your head,
as flashy as platform shoes,
its chromatic basslines, walking
up just ahead of the beat to which you'd
come alive in oceans
of ells and spins and synthesis. Uncle,

Andres Amitai Wilson

Who repeated himself
constantly, while washing endless dishes,
but when asked, was a compendium
of surprises, an encyclopedia brain
with pages and wings and turrets,
ascending up and out
like medieval castles or the expanding
tracks, extending out in all directions from Park Street Station.

The trains you rode
and read, in Boston, in Poland, as far as Australia—the T,
the subways, the streetcars,
and their lilting dance. Once I caught you dancing
to a disco channel somewhere in the thousands on
the cable TV you paid for.

You didn't see me,
but your body popped and locked,
hips shimmied, knees dropped,
shoulders opened—a magical robot,
oiled by the break of beats.

Uncle, you cleaned my grandmother's
behind at twilight so she could die in her own bed.
Uncle, you mastered Kung-Fu
but lost your temper whenever
I disagreed with your unmoored politics.
Look, like so many of us, I barely
had a father, but man

did I have an uncle.

Sunflower

Elaine Joy Edaya Degale

Elaine Joy Edaya Degale

In the Philippines, the reactions to my existence were split: those who regarded Americans as traitorous, self-interested imperialists met me with great discontent, while others responded with inquisitiveness, of which there were many levels. In my mind, I ranked them in accordance with how many personal boundaries were transgressed upon.

"Where are you from?" seemed pretty benign in terms of introductory greetings. Despite the fact that I never really invited such interactions, polite eye contact on my end was alluring enough to commence the impromptu interviews. The initial question was followed by a polite "Are you half, ma'am?" To which I would respond affirmatively and volunteer that it is my mother who is Filipina. Then: "The other half, ma'am?"

"American."

"African, ma'am?"

"American."

"But Americans have blue eyes and blonde hair, like the Hollywood movies, ma'am."

To which I responded with silence.

Some would then ask, "Your mother in the military, ma'am?" Again, always polite, but now at a point of intrusiveness in terms of discerning class status.

"No, not military," I would say. "My mother was a civil engineer and professor here before she left for the States."

"Wow ma'am, where in the States?"

"New York City."

"Like the movies, ma'am?"

"Yes, like the movies."

And it was always this question that didn't make a lot of sense: "Saan ka sa Filipinas, maam?" ("Where in the Philippines is your family living?")

Here, I would proudly beam, "Mindanao."

During this time, the southern provinces of the Mindanao were not a typical place where people aspired for anything like the United States. I could typically tell if the person interviewing me was from the north or south based on how they reacted to this answer. Most people from the capital of Manila regarded Mindanao as backward, poor, and full of hicks. They typically responded with a dishonest smile and horror in their eyes when I said I was from there, because the media had painted Mindanao as dangerous.

They then concluded, "Are you Muslim? Be careful, the food has pork." The conclusion assumed that I must be the kid of a datu, a rich Muslim tribal chief, or some other type of Muslim royalty. This was not true, of course. But there had been times when I would just indulge and pretend to be who people needed me to be in that moment.

"Ang galing naman ng life mo maam, gala-gala lang," they would say. ("Your life seems to be a never-ending vacation. I wish I had that too.")

"Oh, no, no. I'm just passing through," I'd say with a smile.

"Can I get a picture with you?" "Can I get an autograph?" "Can we be penpals?"

I endured variations of this conversation throughout my childhood. These were the conversations I would be greeted with no matter what corner of the world I found myself in—simply existing. Anywhere there was a touch of the Philippine diaspora, the routine sketch that is my life was the same. The same conversation happened in China. The same in Portugal. The same in Spain, France, Curaçao, and Germany. It's a song and dance that is a piece of home wherever I go. To be honest, maybe I invited myself into these conversations when I spoke in Tagalog or Ilonggo every time I heard a Philippine accent embellish English with the tunes of my hometown glory.

Returning to the Philippines as the only Black American person—probably even the last one most people will see in their lifetime—is like being famous in a charming sort of way. The curiosity that random acquaintances regarded me with swung between extremes: some regarded me with immeasurable envy or even hatred, while others idolized me as a source of inspiration that mitigated the great distance of being American versus being a southern Filipino with indigenous roots.

To most in our humble town of Sto. Niño, the United States of America feels worlds away. Too many oceans to cross, too much time to waste, too much money to spend. Every time I returned home more than once a year, the farmers that toiled the fields (which included my extended family) never commented on the weather, as most Americans might. Rather, comments were typically like: "Ay kanami lang gid sa imo daw Marbel lang tana ang America." ("What a charming life of yours, to have the freedom to regard the U.S. as if it were just the next town over.")

I've been flying internationally since I was three and traveling from New York to the Philippines alone (except with plane crew supervision) since I was eleven. Being on sixteen-hour flights and traveling for two days straight to cross the imaginary boundaries, separated into what they called the first, second, and third worlds, has always been normal for me. International demarcations that required visas, saving prodigiously for "show money" to prove I was wealthy enough to be granted a tourist visa, proving that I was fit for travel through medical examinations, marrying for convenience and achieving citizenship, seducing Americans for a shot at the American Dream, were not something that my existence ever required.

I was born American. Abraham Lincoln, Black Civil War heroes, abolitionists, and Martin Luther King Jr. gave their lives for me to enjoy this global privilege.

In the same vein, from an objective standpoint, many Filipinos fought and died so that access to the American Dream inadvertently became solely accessible to the rich and intelligentsia classes of the Philippines. These were things I never had to contemplate as someone born in Long Beach, California. The first time I understood the privilege of being American was when my mom's undocumented friend, Corai, buried her face into my blue passport—the thing that gave me freedom of movement all over the world.

I'm Black, and I am very lucky.

In New York City, to be Black is to be cool, a trendsetter, and this was true of my existence in the Philippines. I felt like royalty and my popularity unnerved me mostly because I just wanted to be left alone. I simply wanted to blend in. But I couldn't. My skin, my hair, was spectacles to be observed, my aura to be suffused by, my life to either be coveted for or imposed upon.

I was viewed as a liberated American, with pubic vulgarity as a crown. I can't tell you how many times a curious person would caress my hair and make comments like, "Look at the purity of this kink!" or "Ooo, such kinky hair!" I didn't understand why sexual terms were always used to describe my hair. Though my classmates in New York City would view me as someone who is prudish and uninformed when it comes to the callings of the flesh, my acquaintances and friends in the Philippines viewed me as an American of liberated values and vulgar humor, because I said things like "shit" and "fuck." Or because my hair reminded them of you-know-what between their legs.

NOVEMBER 23, 2001 - Balikbayans

My belly sank into itself as we descended on the Philippines' capital city. The flight from JFK, including the layover in Korea, was approximately twenty-seven hours long. Upon exiting the airport, the wet kiss of Manila's heat bathed me in unsolicited sweat that drenched my undergarments in ways I don't care to detail. It must be noted that as the plane descended into the green and concrete scenery that divide the rich and poor in the nation's capital, Manila was greeted by a chorus of applause from all the balikbayans, a term for Filipinos returning to the motherland. The scene on the plane was a joyous one. As immigration processes approached, Naomi handed me off to my Uncle Oscar, whose personal connections allowed him entry into the immigration queue.

Immigration was a swarming chaos, saturated with the quiet negotiations of arrivals and the officers tasked with the responsibility and power to stamp the papers that allowed people like me to stay in the country longer. As American citizens, we are only allowed to stay for thirty days. I saw Uncle Oscar insert a one-thousand pesos bill into my passport before handing it to the immigration officer. For a moment, I thought he had forgotten to retrieve it. But when my passport was returned, a balikbayan stamp presented itself on one of the visa pages. This meant that I was good to stay in the country for one year, as opposed to one month. The transaction, which completely escaped me, did not fall short of painting a glow of achievement on my uncle's face.

When I asked why he looked so pleased, he furtively guided me to the baggage claim carousel in response. The silence was uncanny.

"Only great things, Elaine. Great things." My Uncle Oscar winked.

***

When we emerged into the furnace of Manila's scathing sun, Uncle Oscar, completely unfazed by the scorching weather, beamed at his wife with pure excitement.

"We got the balikbayan stamp!" Uncle Oscar told my Tia Alma in failed hushed tones as she busied herself greeting me with kisses and helping me with the luggage.

"That's good, Popsie!" she responded, reflecting his excitement. She placed her hands on my shoulder and smiled widely, "Welcome back Laine. You lost some weight. So sexy mo na ah!" She grabbed the smallness of my waist. "Just a few months ago, we saw pictures of you on Friendster. You were big then. What happened? It's so fast!"

"I only ate chicken ramen for the past month," I replied shyly.

"Anyway, we fly to Mindanao in a few hours. Are you hungry?" Tia Alma took off my backpack and handed it to my cousin, Christian, who looked surprised to be tasked with carrying my bag.

"Thank you, Chris," I smiled. "When we get to the hotel, I will give you your pasalubong!"

Homecoming gifts from the United States were always a novelty that transcended any sort of potential conflict. Pasalubong cured the insanity of conflict in a way that was unmatched. Anything that came from the United States was tantamount to gold. On many occasions, I took the liberty of using American-bought homecoming gifts as items to be pawned in the name of conflict resolution. I'd also lost thirty pounds.

As our car exited Ninoy Aquino Airport, the sweaty mouth of the beast where Ninoy Aquino was assassinated, I was captivated by the small set of hazel eyes glued to my window. With them were delicate hands stained with poverty's demands. She peered at me with a helplessness I'd never encountered before. My inclination to roll down the window and offer her some change was quickly interrupted by my Tia Alma. She hovered her hand over my arm knowingly, with empathy in her eyes.

"Laine, don't. If you roll down your window, more will come, and we will never be able to maneuver our way out of here. You don't want us to accidentally run over them, right?"

My heart hardened and guilt stung my face. The girl hung on the door for a few moments more. Eventually, she started to laugh, and I smiled too.

"Hehe! Negra! Negra!" She pointed and jeered. Her friends came to join her. They joked about me being someone's ugly girlfriend. It became apparent they were no longer interested in money. They must've thought I looked really funny, and this must have made their day somehow.

Elaine Joy Edaya Degale

NOVEMBER 25, 2001 - One Big Bed

The house swarmed with life as I unpacked, and I was happy. So happy! Ah, it felt so good to be home! Since my arrival, my aunts, uncles, cousins, and distant relatives had paid me a visit with tasty treats in tow. All my favorite foods were brought before me. One of them was Mango Float, which is made of graham crackers, condensed milk, and ripened yellow mangoes frozen in cream. Another was unripe mangoes sliced in shrimp paste.

My uncle passed by to drop off the keys to my mother's new van so that I had a ride readily available if I found myself in the mood to go to the town. There wasn't such a thing as privacy when I came home. We all pulled our sleeping mats together to create one big bed and sleep together. As I was still jet-lagged, I listened to everyone and giggled to the gurgling sounds of sleep all through the night.

NOVEMBER 27, 2001 - Lechon Baboy

Have you ever witnessed the slaughter of a pig? My pet piggy, the thing I fed with a baby bottle just this summer, was up for slaughter. I protested this at first, mostly due to guilt. But then I realized that I did not come up with the food chain. The gods did.

Manong Beroy, Uncle Macky, Mayok, and Uncle Boten stood by a giant cauldron of boiling water fanning themselves, drinking ice-cold water. They took off their shirts, and the perspiration of the humid day painted a mosaic of sweat on their bare bodies. One of Piggy's legs was tied to a coconut tree and the preparations for slaughter were in full swing. There was fear in Piggy's eyes, as if she knew what was coming. She had poop all over herself in morbid anticipation. I also wondered—rather I hoped—that she was planning her escape.

Before she was greeted by her impending death, they spoke to her like they did when she was a baby. They bathed her carefully, examined her to make sure she was pure of wounds. The gentler the men were, the more fear flooded her eyes. The stray dogs congregated around her, as if saying their goodbyes. Piggy started to cry.

Mayok found a piece of wood and whacked her over the head with it. She squealed and ran around in the circle that her leash allowed. Tugging, pulling, yearning for freedom. Somehow, the leash loosened, and she broke free after the second whack. They chased her around. She must've been dizzy. As they chased her, they whacked her a couple more times.

She was about 80 pounds, my dear Piggy, and boy did she almost outrun them.

"Kaluoy! Kaluoy!" I cried, running away. The poor thing! My poor thing! But I needed to see how it ended.

They eventually caught her and tied her back to the tree, almost unconscious. The men were glistening from the chase under the blazing sun. Mayok took the knife and jammed it into her throat. She convulsed, cried, and writhed in pain. She tried to escape once more, pulling her tied up leg and bleating before she withered and died. The mangy dogs dispersed by the end of the slaughter, and I wondered if they found this entertaining.

Piggy was laid on the ground with a gaping hole in her throat. They poured boiling water into the wound to disinfect the incision site. They then took a thin blade and scraped the hairs off the pig. They started with the face and worked their way across until her tail. Beroy joked about washing her pussy. He examined and fondled it for a while before pouring hot water into it.

After her body hair was scraped, they took a torch and torched off her nails. The nails fell off like gun casings.

"Bang Bang. Piggy's getting a manicure Elaine, haha!"

Piggy's blood dripped until she was almost white. She kind of looked like a small human to me.

That day I learned—to die is the natural course of things in this grand drama we call life. To be human is to be most powerful. We kill life for food in order to live.

It was Grandma's birthday. To celebrate another year in Grandma's life, Piggy had to die, and she tasted good. We all shared in the bounty of her legacy.

We call this dish "Lechon Baboy."

NOVEMBER 28, 2001 - White, Like Mom

"Do you ever wish to be white?"

"I wish to look like my mother."

"Have you ever heard about homemade bleaching creams?"

Sheila Marie and I spent yesterday afternoon frozen stiff in a homemade bleaching cream we made ourselves. Apparently, after church on Sunday she went into the city to buy the ingredients for the concoction. Marquee White Henna, hydrogen peroxide, grated soap chips (Dove in this case), lemon juice, and Kojic Acid soap. She had inherited the ingredients list from her mother, my Tia Nelfa.

Tia Nelfa had developed a really bad case of eczema, allegedly from the overuse of the whitening concoction. However, when I was in first grade, I vividly remembered my Tia Alma sprawled out naked, waiting for the mixed concoction to dry on her skin. Well, she's pretty and I thought that maybe someday I'd be pretty too. God willing.

An hour later, we continued to stand naked in my bedroom. The clock was ticking audibly and for many moments it felt like we were doing something wrong. Something against the laws of nature. They repeatedly say in church that God makes no mistakes. While I don't think I'm a mistake, maybe my mother's story about my birth can be edited as I grow older. "The Black baby grew up to be more like me, and I'm proud!"

Do I make my mother proud? Maybe this is the magic concoction that would make me more like her. Sheila had convinced me that we would both be a few shades lighter. In my case, I was excited for the possibility of blending in and looking more Filipino. Maybe one day, I could live in a world where people don't tease me for being different. Maybe I'd be more normal. Right?

***

When we were in second grade, my Tia Janet did my hair for a Christmas party. She combed my hair gently until it rose like bread. After a deluge of hairspray and gel, my hair elevated itself to the sky and rested above my head like a crown. I felt very pretty and adorable.

When my classmates saw me, Ritchel took one of the blue ball ornaments from the class Christmas tree and placed it in my hair. As it hung there, he said, "Wow, your hair is like a Christmas tree!"

Some of the kids found it really funny, but I thought it was cool that my hair could be decorated with seasonal objects. I tried returning the gesture, but the ornament fell and crashed to the ground because his hair was too short and straight. Other students started trying to put ornaments in their hair and duly failed.

As crusts of soap chips disbanded themselves from our coat of sin, Sheila Marie began to contemplate other ways to become more beautiful.

"Have you heard of Japanese hair rebonding? Maybe it would work on your hair, and you can have straight hair too."

As Sheila Marie offered this option, I contemplated the times she spent the evenings twisting palm leaves into her sister's hair so she could enjoy a curl pattern similar to mine. Nevertheless, I was intrigued.

"Would it work?" I paused. "On my hair, I mean. Will it go straight?"

"It might. I'm saving up money to get it done myself."

"But your hair is already straight." I stared at the large bundle that sat on top of her head.

"No, it's wavy," she said. "I want it completely straight, like the Sunsilk commercials."

All Filipino Sunsilk commercials featured the same silky straight hair, dark as midnight. The commercials were always of pale-faced women, typically whitened, with a pointy nose, swaying to a corny jingle. Then, towards the end, a random hand would appear on the screen and place a wide-tooth comb on the top of the model's head. The comb would subsequently slide off the hair; smooth, straight, and shiny, like the mane of a well-groomed horse.

My hair was never destined for such a thing. My hair rose towards the sun and sprawled itself—announced itself—and swayed against the direction of a light breeze, opening like an embrace to the world.

Like a sunflower.

allegiance

(poetry collection)

Cianga

blue fever

1960-1965.
the quietest of
nightmares. i awoke
running cold & wet—
my soul, a sorrow in a
trenchcoat

of a body. i was bone-
chilled while a city stunk a
despair
so still, my feet screaming
against gravel
         could've been an ant's footfalls
under the equator's angriest skylight
with all the urgency of a scorned oracle

in the market, i took to
mothers & sons
teaming to secure fufu
by the handfuls
i screamed at their faces, all
shades of disappearing
i grabbed & shook the nearest
body—a child
she shuddered once, then walked away
Kinshasa was a field of gold
Leopoldville was a field of graves

the quietest of nightmare
begins here
watching history move like
cattle to slaughter
an ending world making way
for the money world
i promise i ran
i ran to my father
his two-year-old body unbroken &
dreaming over his mother's lap

i promise, i warned my grandmother
against complacency,
warned her for safety

    – my voice could've
          been air

i promise i went to the caves
i dug the coltan with my teeth

i spit
bluegold
at the first
overseer i
saw
i overturned
carts &
mountains
of coltan
        – my raw & red body failed
everywhere i bled; a child
swallowed a mine to become valuable
everywhere i screamed, a city
drowning echoed silence

Cianga

the money world
the money world
printed bible verses
to replace machetes
so angry, we cry
so moved by God, we cry
bitter, bitter blues
hues unnatural on skin
blues on limbs, but it's never been hotter
this coltan fever
this nightmare so
quiet, it is made
of history

this period, the world saw
congo for its potential
a people to be pocketed, a kingdom to be farmed
my father would
eventually run, a cusp
baby born between a
dying country & the
illusion of choice
he must not have run very far
his eyes are always here & away
whatever he buys for me is never blue

marketfield

2021.
the mothers of Kinshasa are rising
a stampede of twenty thousand

demand their right to open shop
they're all shades of black & angry

violently hungry
the lady of edible clay sheds her shawl

competitor, the lady of chili eggs
coats her nails red. everything is alive

and wants to stay that way
Kinshasa is a seascape of delicious rage

i am tossed in a myriad of dyes & fish
& *watch your back, kin, we must win*

i look for the voice, but everywhere are songs
of threats & courage. everything is

beautiful until i understand the words
 they want us gone in the name of rehabilitation

what's that even mean? i sell to feed my son
i offer my zeal to the wind & the sweaty

twenty thousand—i inherit their rage

Cianga

i try to join with an off-key cry

like i'm gonna protest loud enough
to rattle the closed gates, shatter the metal

but my voice is paper next to their blades
watch your back, kin. don't delay us

the mothers of Kinshasa are rising
and i have nothing to offer them

i can only watch in reverence
at the way one secures a bag of fufu

on her head, swings a machete &
keeps her daughter's feet from the soil

all while the governor sits & prays & eats if i
    cannot myself break the gates or his peace

i can at least reach out, grab the closest arm
speak in *lingala* as broken as my voice

in 2024, the governor will be arrested for fraud
in 2024, the market lives

a refugee's life's worth

time my father walked with those rebels
time that biked missed me
time i first kissed a girl, the minutes between our breaths
time i'm prayed over like my skull's housing demons
time i was born, after the failed child
time my father ran for a volleyball &
continued to play, despite his fall time
i first swipe my EBT
time we speak on gender &
   Vish says he *honestly doesn't*
really give a shit
time i spend to smile
time Lumumba said *Africa will write its own history*
time i searched for congolese
history &
   find no congolese authors
time i take my first antipsychotic
time i'm told i can't swim cause i'm black
time i watch *Insidious* & dream of
the red-skulled demon for weeks
time before Lumuba's assassination
time between days
time I hold my pee without a toilet in sight
time my nephew cried, then laughed. then cried again
everytime I cook chicken, steam the fat,
drain the impurities &
toss the skin
time I squish an ant
time work grows hands & sorrows

Cianga

time I teach a boring class – Zou'd say, *there's life in between*
all'at—
>   like we're steak fat
time i won't wake up
time i hold my baby nephew's pulse to my own
time is something like Lumumba's Congo—
>   always arriving always out of reach
& everything matters before it doesn't

>   all of it – i cried & ate & threw up &
>   drew my nephew Gabriel's arms so close
>   i could've been his mother in another life my own mother
>   won't stop texting & i am running out of time before i have
>   to eat again. did i even remember to hydrate? i fell out of
>   something like love—all of it

 barely a week of time between it all
in other words, a lifetime
& between it all,
i must have lived

fields of madness

in the year of my birth, my father saw

      a city disappear before the world. again & again.
      the children drank mud
      the elders broke bones over bread
      the able & angry took to arms &
      steel & leapt over borders waving
      photographs before flags only to find

madness.

cities of empty houses
cities of needles & rope
cities of bleached trees
cities of seated folk
cities of endless, stupid questions

yes, you starved, but were you a communist?

father worked for the red cross   so mad he later
begged them for asylum
and later begged to see his kids
and even later begged to be let out

madness.

i'm able & angry enough to leap into congress
my own stupid questions in row

      how come we got land only for grass?
      if we hate genocide so much,

Cianga

       how come we've been through so many?

i've got a city dirty in my nails

       all red pill blues. all running to an end
       only to find a door to the beginning like
       the war never really ended or even begun
       like we were kings, you know? i heard it
       or dreamt it like our apocalypse is reborn at
       the world summit – kings, man – i could
       disappear & no city will stop talking enough
       to notice i was gone till bills need to be paid

there's a stray cat in my yard that won't leave
too plump for the streets, it prowls my lawn
no use in begging
no use for this grass

but in it's drooling & circling, i see
the first signs of madness

fields of faces

for my citizenship interview
my agent brings my everything in one folder

i'm so full i could burst over his table & fly
in a sea of faces waiting for their names i see
junpei! we worked together once on some art
he's so happy he wishes his husband could be
here i am already with my right hand across
my chest & alone in mourning something
no one in this sea of faces seem to be honest
like they're scared the president will stop his
speech & snatch their certificates from their
hands but *junpei!* he's next to me again & his
smile has faded, only a little, & i don't think
                    i'll ever see these people again, at least a name

                    surely, i would remember at least that

i take my oath alone
i leave the building with nothing but a face

Ordinary Magic
(poetry collection)

Blessing Odunyemi

Blessing Odunyemi

Masquerade (Eégún)

Sure. Wars are battled in your womb.

Yes. You scurry like the cockroach

to safety. Of course. You mind cracks

from unwelcome hands. Eh-heh. You fall

into vats of hot oil and leave with no burns.

Indeed. You make banquets

out of mouldy bread and mercury fish.

Certainly. You take 100 lashes of horsewhip

on your back and wake to unbroken skin.

Sure, you bathe me, baby

Dress me up and make me the terror that I am

Envelop me in your lunar softness

Softness that we know would shred

My cloth and the man behind it.

But you will die if you look upon me, woman.

I, the one who hides behind heavy mask,

will be your undoing.

**Eégún: the Yoruba term for "Masquerade", / a masked and costumed individual who is representative of sacred things.*

Àkúdàáyà*

And he, stuck in purgatory
Shook the line viciously
For he had plans
Great plans
For his given life
But his life was cut into half

So, he found himself a loophole
In a name - Forgotten -
A woman of old
He asked, begged, pled
for accolades to make him credible
Then, he fed from Power's teat
Power, he did have aplenty

But he indeed had not had enough
He'd been enriched—lifted
Had gold   singed from dust
Children   born from expired loins
Glory   hunted like prey—
Stained his teeth in decayed decadence

Then, he felt death's piercing ring
Impending and wore cotton in his ears
When they found falseness in his likeness
He built armies with trigger hands
Because death's bell was ever near

He set fire to his Fatherland

*Àkúdàáyà – *a Yoruba myth about a person who has died, usually suddenly or prematurely, but whose spirit walks amongst the living in a different location.*

Blessing Odunyemi

Grandma's Emissaries

We walk side by side
In sync, in perfect time
We have but a few moments
Amongst your living

You throw a feast for your dearly departed
Well, dust-to-dust tongue deserves a taste
Like she did from the chronic comfort
Of her living room parlour
Somebody has to check for maggi

We walk side by side
In sync, in perfect time
Our noses aren't for breath
But homing in on aromas

We soon find ourselves
Within your crowds of starving faithful
Pushing to the front

We first seek payment by entertainment
At your expense

We watch side by side
In sync, in perfect time
Your cauldron roiling
On the firewood

Olopo performs great feats for her audience
Transforming her fingers into scoop
Plopping dollops of bean potion
On the simmering surface of hot *ororo*
We watch them drown, then float

We smell side by side
In sync, in perfect time
Anaemic fritters that catch a tan
Thanks to Maillard's Midas Touch

She knows when to remove and drain them
The hungriest draw closer, risking coal lungs
But heat makes scent intoxicating
Small sacrifice for what's to come
They are rewarded with paper-wrapped morsels

We shout side by side
In sync, in perfect time
"Give us akara!"
Authoritative imperative

Our demand mismatches
Corporeal juvenile frames
You're wise to not question our manners
For we are older than your ancestors
Olopo prepares a fresh batch for us

Blessing Odunyemi

We sit side by side
In sync, in perfect time
As you all observe in silence
Our mystical presence

Before long, our hands are filled
We prepare to take the piping hot bounty
To her new forever parlour
That no living being can see
You wave us off with thank yous

We take our leave side by side
In sync, in the most perfect time
To your love, for her verdict
Voiced through daylight butterflies*

Iyawo Kekere (Small Wife)*

There is a lot riding on you
Youth. You are the key to our
Financial security

You know how this dance goes
You have seen your friends
Your sisters go through the motions

It is a production line
Be desirable
Seen. Barely heard
Epitome of modesty
Be present
Right place, right time
Let him notice you
Do whatever it takes for him to notice you
But not too much

Let him make the next move
He will ask about you
Send someone to call you over
Here, your work is hard but easy
All you have to do is be meek
Yet leave him wanting
Lead him into your family home
To greet us, the elders
And asks for your hand

Blessing Odunyemi

We'll exchange you for dowry
We reared you
We shall set a high price
Finally, you will be carried away
To your husband's house
To give him children
And his children will be many
The more a wife births
The more she is loved
And his wives are many

You aren't the first
You might not be the last
And Quarrel will knock
Travelling door to door
Waiting for one scorned to answer
And you will lose your last name
Go by your firstborn's first
Your youth will fade
But you will be happy
For you will have brought us riches
For you will have avoided shame

Communion

(Setting: Living room. Red carpet scorched
by equatorial sun.
Mirrored table – reflects – blinds daughter
who squeezes foetal form into palm
of an exhausted settee. Opposite
father, focused.
Scored by cautionary tales
in shades of Nollywood.)

On a day of no consequence,

Baba gave me coconut—cursed.

It had no juice and no crunch.

Chewed like gum. Gulp.

I thought it was body

nourishing treat,

but he tried to fill me

with his blood

to turn me from offspring to object

that loved him wholly, only

to become knife that rips

through familial fabrics so mama – mortal enemy

finally died of a broken heart

and set him free.

Instead, at dawn,

my stomach formed a knot.

Pain punished me for believing

virtue lined malice.

His spell left my body

in violent retches

that sunk to the bottom of our WC.

The House on Bar Street

(poetry collection)

Christian Curet

Christian Curet

The Masks We Wear

I wear this mask to protect them, to make them feel safe
from the fear they've decided not to face.
It's not a virus they hate, but a sickness of the mind.
What I'm protecting them from is me and mine.

I can't breathe.

My brothers and sisters didn't protest
the masks,
we've worn them since they brought us
in clamps.
Shackled, chains forged by ignorance
and hate.
Getting whipped, beaten, killed, our
only hope escape.
To save our lives we bore masks of
obedience and deference,
'cause we thought our allegiance would
make a difference.
That if we looked as if we feared them,
they would let us be,
but those masks couldn't hide our pain
hung from every tree.

I can't breathe.

We still wear masks. Grotesques carved
by anger, sculpted by hate.
Still being beaten, imprisoned by
millions, at a much higher rate

than our White neighbors, like those
who cry "All Lives Matter"
while kneeling on our backs, our necks,
to climb their own ladder.
Some of us shield our faces with
kindness, the moral high ground
to seem like we are above the fray, but we are drowned
in the sea of Black and Brown faces on the screen
one after another, jailed or killed, yet they remain unseen
by those who hate them the most, just a statistic;
their descriptions of us, always sadistic.
And I know, most of you
want to do
everything to
help us through
struggles till we're all black and blue
together.
And please know
I love you, though

I still can't breathe.

Through my own mask of fear, my soul is weighed
down by thoughts like, "Will I be unmade?"
Walking in a park, jogging, buying candy?
No crime is too small for my life to be
snuffed out like a black candle summoning back
the demons of our past; the whip's crack
echo through my bones. So, I wear my mask
of civility, of patience, of fear—all so I can ask
for my own life, please sir. I can't breathe.
I just want to breathe.
And be free.

Christian Curet

Sandra Bland
Trayvon Martin
Sean Reed
Tamir Rice
Oscar Grant
Michael Brown
Stephon Clark
Dante Parker
Walter Scott
Anthony Baez
Ahmaud Arbery
Breonna Taylor
Philando Castile
Samuel Dubose
Freddie Gray
Eric Garner
Alton Sterling
Atatiana Jefferson
Botham Jean
George Floyd
Mario Arrenales
Patrick Lyoya
Jayland Walker
Donovan Lewis
Micheal Ramos
Johnathan Price
Derrick Kittling
Sean Monterosa

Say their names. They deserved to be heard. And still breathe.

The House On Bar Street

It was summer at the house on Bar Street, and
at five or six I was just learning about heat.

My mother had given my brother and me some relief,
a few slices of watermelon each to eat.

So juicy, we ate them outside,
our shirts joyfully tossed behind us,
a pile of whites and cares.

We sat there on the front porch, spitting
black seeds
across the sidewalk and into the street.
A competition to see who could offend
the furthest.

Next door, the torn-down old home whose ruin
was our next target, an exploration of nails and dust.
A mother's nightmare, a child's dream.

We ate until little bellies bulged with sweetness,
dribbled with juice, ached with laughter.

Two old men wearing VFW hats walked down the sidewalk.
Ghosts of cheap beer and smoke trailed after them
as they walked past our glistening pile of offenses.
Looking at my brother and me, they just shook their heads.

Christian Curet

I couldn't hear what they said when they
passed,
but their laughter echoed after them.
Their faces and words hooded by war,
foreign and domestic.
Soldiers, just following orders.

It wasn't until much later that I knew why those men laughed.
Their sheeted costumes remained long
after they became bitter specters,
but the watermelon was still cold, and good.

My brother and I kept eating the slices of sweet.
Two brown berries enjoying a summer treat.

Her Teeth are White Like Ice

Michael Eshetu

Michael Eshetu

"

Eskkista, Esskista! Mickey, Mickey! Come for dance!"
The corners of Sara's mouth stretched wide as her native tongue transitioned to English, giving a softness to her vowels.

"You have to teach me!" I said, making an excuse to stay towards the back of the crowd surrounding the makeshift dancefloor. I stayed put as my aunty came to the rescue, entering the middle of the floor to join Sara.

Their shoulders moved up and down in a traditional Ethiopian dance. The group clapped in rhythm with the *masenko* chords, a weird blend of a violin and ukelele. Everyone's clothes, including the national dress, merged into blurry and white as we celebrated Saint Michael's Day. I peered around the room to make sure my claps were on beat, occasionally softening them in case they were off. The familiar *"Eskkist"* chant repeated as aunty ran out of steam, just in time for my cousin Sam to jump onto the dancefloor.

Sam was on another level, raising and lowering his shoulders, one at a time, two at a time, throwing in head movements from side to side. The chants and clapping grew in decibels. Sweat beads formed at the corners of his receding hair line, but you couldn't help but keep your gaze on how he moved. Sara and Sam's eyes locked, each unable to stop their smiles. They were in sync with the clapping in the background.

Photos of family on the walls began to shake, and I worried about the urn that sat in the left corner. My breaths drew tight, oxygen struggled to pass my throat. Hunched over, I realised the clapping in the background was now ringing in my ears. To get to the sandy porch, my legs stumbled through the sea of white clothes—cousins, uncles and aunties. The skin around my forearm turned red from pinching, my attempt to distract myself from incessant coughing and an inability to breathe.

"Cold, huh?"

"Awo, yes. Very." The chill of the wind stung the sweat around my temples; words fell between coughs and deep inhalation.

"It's beautiful, yes? Eskista? Ethiopian dance?"

"The most beautiful, Uncle," I said. As he sat on the wooden chairs, I offered a smile, slowly rising to an upright position, sucking in the cold air.

"Your dad was very good at this dance."

A cool breeze blew my warm breath towards the tach bet, the low house. The chickens seemed like a suitable place to rest my stare and practice the mindfulness techniques that were a staple in therapy. My therapist was always on about how I frequently drifted off, struggling to remain present.

"Terefe taught me when I was kid, Mickey," he said, latching onto my forearm to grab my attention. It worked and we faced one another, which made it more difficult to conceal my laboured breathing. "He was good, but too high." Uncle raised his spare hands above his head to communicate how tall my father was; his other hand clutched my arm, keeping me captive.

"Mickey, will you help finish church building?"

A pause filled the icy air before I agreed. Simultaneously, I added pinch marks on my arms. "Of course, Uncle."

"Please, please. This is important." His stern nodding accompanied his plea. Uncle's long beard, having hints of grey, glistened under the porch lamp that sometimes dimmed in power in the Ethiopian's rural hills.

"You know this tree, don't you?" Uncle said, pointing to the outline of a Eucalyptus that stood thirty metres from the house. "Yes, yes, this was brought in by your country. Menelik, our emperor, loved this tree. Now, they are everywhere.

"Aus-tra-li-a!" Uncle tapped my forearm to the beat of the syllables, syncing them with the background claps. "Ha-be-sha!" He repeated with the same tapping. "You know what this means, yes?" His smile beamed through his beard.

I nodded, feeling uneasy that my uncle's grasp remained, and I breathlessly worked to recover from the offense that he thought I didn't know Habesha was the word for Ethiopian people.

Sara's voice burst onto the porch and quickly trailed off as she hurried back towards the house made of mud. "Mickey, come back. Aunty is dancing, come!"

Freeing my arm from Uncle, I followed Sara into the house. The blur and white returned, family clapping in unison as my 60-year-old Aunty danced with Sara, her daughter. Both of them were draped in matching sets of white dresses with green, yellow, and red accents on the collars and cuffs.

Sam worked to catch his breath at the back of the circle, dapping the corners of his forehead with napkins. We signalled one another with raised eyebrows before he exited the circle. Minutes later he brought over two plastic cups of homemade beer. He and I snuck out the back of the house, into the cold, avoiding the older family members' errand requests.

The music continued as the two of us stood under the stars.

"Cheers." Sam raised his cup, mimicking my Australian accent, only to sound British. I met his impersonation with my own cheers before we both took a large gulp. "You are high like him."

"Who? Terefe?" I asked.

Snickers filled the air; Sam understood my joking about dads' name.

"You called him Terefe?" asked Sam.

"No, no. I wouldn't."

"Good, Mickey. You should not."

The two of us looked at the flickering light at the front of the tach bet as we sipped the beer from our cups.

"You're short, but you like to fight, yeah?" Our fists raised in jest.

Earlier that day, Sam drove us from Addis Ababa to our grandfather's land, navigating wildlife, potholes, and my motion sickness. We had stopped halfway at Debre Birhan. Sam went to retrieve emnet, a powdered incense used in church ceremonies; the word translates as faith in English.

My light skin signaled my foreignness and potential for money. So, on the walk back to the car, a large Ethiopian in worn clothes didn't take kindly to my refusal to give.

Sam recalled this moment, mocking the man from earlier. "Give money, lightskin," he said, hunching over with laughter. He placed his hand on my shoulder. "One punch, yeah?"

"One from me, one from you, Sam."

"He will be dead."

Sam had stepped in to have a word with the guy who was double his size; he was ready to fight. "You have problem with my brother? Zorbel, get out of here. Thief!"

We finished off the last bit of the home brewed sediment. My eyes landed on Sam's arm, still resting on my shoulder. His face was like mine—soft around the eyes but sharp in the jaw and cheeks.

He put himself on the line when I had walked away from that guy. The image was vivid along with the palpable love and care Sam showed for me. Moments after feeling insecure, having not stepped up to the plate, I realised the significance of that moment and what it meant.

"I could have taken him on my own though," I said. My foot rested on the small fence that edged the side of the back door. I shot Sam a brief glance before breaking eye contact.

"Of course, Brother. Mickey, son of Terefe!"

We snickered. Sam was aware of the context of that comment; his pause before replying reflected just that.

Sam gestured to return inside. Hesitating for a moment, I followed, simultaneously sucking in a deep breath.

Inside, Sam's mum quickly dragged him into a chore. Being the family's youngest meant he was called upon the most—to clean, prepare food, to do the heavy lifting, including the building of the mud house from the ground up during his few days off.

Michael Eshetu

The mud was compact, but specks could be seen on the walls if you looked close enough. Among the specks was a photo of dad from when we first came here years ago. In the photo, Dad wore a serious expression. Next to that picture was an image of him and me in our wetsuits on a surf in Australia not too long ago.

I caressed the edges of the frame, studying the rough water that was behind us in the picture.

"Mickey, this is a good photo, yes?"

"It is nice," I replied.

Sara eyes the first photo. "When you and your dad were first here, Mickey?"

"Yeah," I replied, softly.

"You had fun, yes? Remember the thieves?" Sara asked, amused. "Too much tej, too much honey wine. I was drunk."

"They steal the money!" she teased, mocking his words from that memory.

"Looking back on it—I think the wine made me overreact." My accent softened as the sentence became more complex in English.

"Thief! Thief!" Sara pointed and grabbed at her stomach, laughing.

I felt bad about that night so many years ago. I was too drunk to calculate a simple bill and ended up calling the waitress a thief in Amharic. This greatly amused my family.

My gaze darted back and forth between Sara and the photo. I feigned a smile, but was unsure if my facial muscles could endure.

The family continued to dance and sing loudly in the background; I was forced to lean in to hear Sara as she spoke.

"Mickey, no girlfriend? You are old man now." She playfully punched me with loose shoulders. I grabbed her shoulders as we playfully wrestled.

"I have three years 'til I am thirty. Give me a chance."

A few family members glanced back from the dance floor while Sam shook his head jovially at us. He returned with a tray of honey wine.

Meanwhile, Sarah continued. "Remember you scared from cow?"

My grip tightened again. My cousin deliberately—yet playfully—kept embarrassing me about my first visit years ago. She wriggled free from my hold, but my mind trailed to the memory.

We'd taken a cow through the valley and up the mountain to be slaughtered and eaten for Saint Michael's Day. Uncle steered the resistant cow with a makeshift lead and collar made of rope. My cousins, Dad, and I trailed behind until the beast freed itself from its noose. It charged towards me while I was on the edge of a cliff. I remember looking at the 30-metre drop to nothing on my left.

The cow's eyes and stride were intense. As he got closer, all I could think to do was jump out of its way—to the right, away from the cliff's edge.

I hit the side of the mountain; my white Ethiopian clothing turned brown with dirt. The cow didn't make it past Dad who took a huge hit to the chest and legs but managed to wrangle the beast to the ground while uncle put the lead back on.

After we arrived at the church in the cave, we prayed and thanked God for our opportunity to eat fresh beef with the freshest injera we had ever tasted. Our legs were thankful for a rest after the 5-kilometre trip up and down the rural hillside. That night, Aunty scrubbed my clothes until they were white again.

Sara's voice snapped me out of my trance; my eyes were still fixed on Dad's portrait.

"Your dad wouldn't scare from this!" Sara smirked, searching for a reaction before she became distracted by a new song with a faster tempo.

Our youngest cousin leapt into the middle of the blurry and white dance circle. His shoulders weightless; he pranced around, playing up to the crowd. My presence waned, however. The surf photo dragged me back again. A cough escaped; I prepared for the constriction that would follow, but Sam's timely interruption halted the familiar anxiety attack.

"He is funny guy," Sam said, gesturing toward our cousin while drawing circles around his own temples.

Our cousin would likely be considered autistic in a westernised society. The facilities to test for this in the middle of rural Africa weren't exactly prevalent.

"Remember he said he went to brothel… and didn't use condom?"

"He is crazy, Sam."

Years prior we'd been walking up the steep hill to the nearest town for a beer and a game of pool when Cousin admitted this to us. Sam had heard some whispers from our aunty and wanted to see if they were true. Our cousin quickly verified the stories with a tangent about how great it felt, and his plans to return promptly. He left the part out about his mum dragging him by his ear to the local clinic to get checked for HIV. He would be rubbing the top of his ears for weeks afterward, and we would forever be scratching our heads at our younger cousin.

"Watch him, Mickey."

My cousin jumped up and down as the claps expedited. Sam and I moved away from the photos towards the middle of the crowd. The mud house felt small; the top of the roof deposited brown flakes into my afro.

Cousin's arms were loose, and his legs were following suit. I tried to imagine what it would feel like to dance without weight, without heaviness. My throat tightened as I watched my first cousin—the son of my dad's sister.

We joined the jumping and shoulder raises, throwing off any specks of mud from our shoulders. Sam egged me on, but my eyes were only on my cousin in the heart of the circle. He soon called Sara in. Both their feet connected with the ground. They belonged in the centre at that moment. Sam and I pushed forward, right there at the front of the dancefloor, having the best view in the house.

"Esskista, Esskista!" Sara danced in sync with our cousin, upping the ante. She was met with an increase of cadence, rhythm, and poetry. Claps intensified as cousin began the next part of the entertainment, a series of serenading.

"Is he going to sing again?"

"Yes, Mickey, he will sing for Sara. Just watch and hear."

Our cousin—the one on the spectrum—chanted raucously to overcome the clapping. His eyes never rested on one spot, but danced around the room. Almost looking possessed, but not malevolent. The chants were short and simple, mostly about how beautiful or smart someone was. Everyone was eager to see what cousin would come up with for Sara.

"Sara! Sara! My sister!"

"Awo." The group replied yes in unison.

"Sara! Sara! My sister!"

"Awo!"

"Sara! Sara! Sister!"

"Awo!"

"Sara! Sara! Her teeth are white like ice."

"Awo!"

"Sara! Sara! Her teeth are white like ice."

"Awo!"

"Sara! Her teeth are white like ice."

"Awo!"

"Her teeth are white like ice."

"Awo!"

"Her teeth are white like ice."

"Awo!"

We snickered, remembering the first time our cousin said that in 2019; it was infectious. And even though I didn't know what it meant back then; the love was obvious.

Sara left the dance centre sweaty and content, joining us, adding a new splash of white with a pop of colour. Upon her departure, the tempo and rhythm changed. Cousin then decided where the Masenko chords would take him next. Everyone kept clapping, while Cousin paraded around the centre until he'd found his next song. He waited for the right moment, a break in the chords to begin.

"Mickey!" he yelled. The crowd erupted, looking for me, the tall light skin boy from overseas who would meet their looks with a nervous smile.

"Awo!" the crowd responded.

"Mickey!" The gestures came for me to enter the circle before a sharp push from Sam landed me in the centre. It was now my turn.

"Awo!"

First, we danced; my eyes scouring the room. Cousin led the way. Copying him was difficult, and it was clear I was out of practice.

"Mickey, son of Terefe, son of Terefe!"

"Awo!"

"Mickey, son of Terefe, son of Terefe!"

"Awo!"

"Mickey, son of Terefe. His land!"

"Awo!"

"Mickey, son of Terefe. His land!"

"Awo!" The crowd's cadence and decibels grew.

"Mickey, son of Terefe. His people!"

"Awo!"

"Mickey, son of Terefe. His people!"

"Awo!"

"Mickey, son of Terefe. HABESHA!"

"Habesha, awo!" The crowd switched the response ever so slightly.

"Mickey, HABESHA!"

"Habesha, awo!"

"Mickey, ours!"

"Awo!"

"Mickey, son of Terefe!"

"Awo!"

Tears filled my eyes. Cousin left the centre for a second and grabbed the urn that sat in the left corner of the room, chanting one last time. He signalled for the room to stop for a moment of silence before belting out his last line.

"Mickey, son of Terefe. Son of the hero! HABESHA! Ours!"

He was met with the emphatic awo from our family, but my mouth couldn't reply; my dancing stopped.

The family surrounded me, but their sounds muffled, like they were underwater. Mindfulness techniques were of no use now. Air would not pass through my throat. My mind returned to the rough waters of that beach only months ago. My fingers tried to pull the wetsuit away from my neck that was no longer there.

I remembered Dad paddled further and further away. His surfboard returned with two struggling swimmers.

He had yelled out to me, his head bobbing in between white capped waves. "Take them in, Mickey!"

I rushed them to shore, my head frequently looking back over my shoulder through the rough waters. The swimmers latched onto the rope of my board.

Back at shore, the two stayed in the care of a couple. I quickly headed back out, paddling harder than ever, my head crashing into the whitewash. The horizon crept closer, but Dad was nowhere to be seen.

The pressure against my ribs forced out coughs. Seagulls circled as shout after shout fell solely on their ears, before my voice cracked and failed.

I dove down into the water, but he was nowhere to be seen. Hours passed and a search continued with the rescue team deep into the night. We all came up empty, emerging from the water shivering and alone. The haunting of why I didn't go with him was the only thing that surfaced.

***

Michael Eshetu

I replayed everything in the months that followed; returning to the beach, paddling towards the horizon, wondering if I could keep going until my arms would give up. Just maybe Dad would appear, or we would end up in the same place—maybe for a dance and some honey wine. I prayed that just beyond the horizon, the land-locked borders of Ethiopia migrated east to become a coastline, a destination I could paddle to. Then, and maybe then, the muscles surrounding my smile would have a break, and the need to conceal the panic and anxiety attacks would be few and far between.

"Mickey, are you there?" Sara's hand rested on my shoulder as I shielded my face to hide my tears. I had somehow ended up in the middle of the crowd. She wrapped her arms around me, taking me to the back of the circle and out of the mud house.

"Izo, Mickey, it's ok."

***

Sam joined us as we made our way to the tach bet. My head firmly hit the pillow on the single bed; my head spun. The music continued for another half hour before it came to a slow stop. We slept among the chickens coming in and out of the low house and were woken at the crack of dawn by the roosters.

The three of us rose, skipped breakfast, and walked to the St. Michael's cave church by the cliff five kilometres from home. I balanced as best possible without the use of my hands which were firmly wrapped around the urn. The paths were jagged, muddy, and hilly. Between the panting, not much was said between us. We arrived at the front of St. Michael's church, greeted by the trademark green-painted rocks and water streams, running down the cave's face. It was the same place the cow escaped years before. We stood briefly, taking it in, unsure if we'd all be in the same place again.

"It was his dream to build a church like our great grandfather did. He was so close."

I opened the lid, my hands shaking as I tried to sign the crucifix across my chest and head. The lid slipped in my hands and Sam quickly caught it, holding tightly. I thrust the urn forward, letting the breeze move through its contents, piloting them into the valley below.

Sara took the empty urn that previously housed the emnet sourced in Debre Birhan. Crouched, I covered my eyes for mere seconds. I felt the hands of both cousins on my back.

"Faith, Mickey," Sam said as he touched the incense between his thumb and index finger that didn't make it into the valley.

Afterwards, we sat with our legs dangling over the cliff, not saying much. We didn't return to our grandad's until nightfall.

***

Sam drove us through the night, through the fog, back to the capital. He left the engine running as I collected my belongings and said bye to the family. Sara cried on the way to the airport. I was quick to tell her off like Dad did the first time we'd departed years before.

"If you cry, we won't come back." She and I both teared up. Snot flew out my nose—half sobbing, half happy. We embraced for longer than ever at the front of Addis Ababa's airport.

"Just stay with us Mickey. Ewedahalu. We love you."

Thoughts about staying in Ethiopia—leading an easier life, using my savings—had come to mind. And although it wasn't ever said, taking care of this family would now be an inheritance from dad. But I couldn't fulfill my role in this family if I stayed. I'd help Sam get his first new car so he could continue driving but would likely never see the inside of his car. I'd help Sara while she completed her master's program in accounting but wouldn't celebrate her graduation with her. I'd get Sam the braces he desperately needed, unsure if I'd see his smile in person again. It was stressful at times, and it was something to be cherished. I was able to help, even if it meant I ate canned tuna and rice for that month.

"Come back soon Mickey, son of Terefe. Habesha man!" Sara yelled out. Her teeth beamed in the night. "Check bag, Mickey!"

I waved passing through the airport doors.

At the gate, I rifled through my bag only to see the photo of dad and I surfing; the specks of mud clinging to the top of the frame. Then the memory of one of our last conversations surfaced.

"That song means your teeth are white like snow, not ice, Mickey. We just don't have a word for snow in Amharic, specifically."

"I think I like it as ice though, it sounds different, but it just fits. Belongs."

That memory would make its way into the Victorian mornings that were cold, where the imaginary wetsuit would be tight around the collar; where there was a want to paddle into nothingness until my arms gave out. In those moments, my refuge was received in the photos of Sam, Sara, and Dad. And just after brushing my teeth, I'd stretch the corners of my mouth and sing the lines:

"Tir swa berado."

"Her teeth are white like ice."

Metamorphosis
Wounds, Wars, and Wings

War is Not Why I Carried You

Nicole Doyley

Nicole Doyley

War is not why I carried you
in my womb
in my arms
in my heart when you left for school.

War is not why I comforted you
when you couldn't sleep
when you fell from your bike
when your heart broke with unrequited love.

War is not why I prayed for you
that you'd emerge into the world unscathed
that you'd find a friend worthy of you
that you'd marry a woman whose love came close to mine.

War is not why I kissed you
on your newborn head
on your little boy cheek
on your nearly grown face.

War is Not Why I Carried You

I didn't carry you to one day welcome you home with
a shattered mind
a shattered limb
a shattered life.

I didn't carry you to receive a triangle flag and gun salute.
I didn't carry you to hear sad stories of your courage.
I didn't carry you to receive a letter, a phone call,
a "Sorry for your loss, ma'am."

I didn't carry you to one day hear,
"Well, we really didn't need that war anyway."

What would happen if the mothers of the world all said,
"War is not why I carried you?"

Melanin Child

Jamil Anuva

Jamil Anuva

Melanin Child

Melanin Child, swaddled in tradition

clutched securely in mother's bosom

Burgeoning with bass, ngoma drums electrify rib cage

Originating a rapturous rhythm that moves beings to blossom

Rites enacting inscription of knowledge upon blank pages

Now and forevermore, omniscient lineages illuminate passage

and if your footing should falter or focus becomes a skewed view

set sights to your roots, for they are the compass to you.

Melanin Child, sculpted from the best offerings

no other clay nor kiln contests

Rays from the sun equate to unadulterated power

As alluring radiance exudes from skin, hair, and eyes

Instinctively visionary, presented absent confinement

Superior displays of brilliance beyond belief, indeed

Explorative creations, inexplicable by contemporary progression

Debased IQ remains perpetually unparalleled by AIs

through it all

    remember how rich the very land beneath your feat

as it affords the essentials

unlike any forgery of man's feeblest attempts.

Melanin Child

Melanin Child, interrupted by a disruptive force
Strewn through displacement, migration, or place of birth
Time
        shifts culture and ideations compulsorily
Oh, Gullah Geechee, Haitians—even Jamaicans—lament
Language and heritage proliferated across seas and continent
Egregiously pillaged, plundered, all the while belittled in worth
Nefarious British museums underhandedly arrest your arts
The world, grows wealth, undermining your diamonds
leaving you in uprooted uncertainty, thriving through setbacks
forced to make home away from homes
according to… plotted setbacks!

Melanin Child, as you dance through the pain

paint murals of vividly contrasting hues

Alluding to varying juxtapositions on a singular plane

But never truly alone; the entire diaspora, your tribe

Unmet, thousands of kilometers apart

Still yet, you are akin to kin

Eagerly aching for a connection, superseding synthetic

Dually mixed as oils and water-based media

inhabiting the same frame

lights and darks giving depth and range

all playing roles in the unveiling of an immaculate image.

Jamil Anuva

Melanin Child, return home with heritage in tow

with an air of self-actualization

Resurfacing, is that resounding reverberation of

                                rhythmic resonance

Endlessly & electrically reminded of the potential in your physic

Though as if surgically implanted by Dr. Daniel Hale Williams—

Unabridged,

      empowered with indignation such as Toussaint Louverture

Revel in knowing Nanny & The Maroons of Accompong

Negus / Nigist—for these are written in DNA

and thus, cannot be stripped away.

The Kito Story

Y Kendall

Y Kendall

He was only two when he disappeared. His pictures show a big, sweet-natured grin, glittering with baby teeth, the same smile that charmed the face of his twin sister and half-brother. All three bore the same misty brown curls typical of biracial babies, with the same peachy bisque skin color.

All three had the same father, Archie, a tall, still-fit, failed former pro athlete with rich skin tones of bittersweet chocolate. Archie indiscriminately scattered his progeny throughout southern Oklahoma, like some dystopian Johnny Appleseed. All three children had mothers of a similar Southern type: skin with the pale, pasty grubbiness of unhealthy eating, stringy hair floundering between blonde and brown, their leaden bodies made shapeless through incessant indolence and relentless fecundity—women whose only attraction for the Black men who bedded them was the formerly forbidden fruit of their white skin. Yes, these three babies were much the same and should have had much the same lifelines. But with one event, Atropos would sever their fates.

Kito's mother, Suellen, waited eighteen months after the twins were born before contacting their father about their existence. She probably wouldn't have bothered, but the State of Oklahoma requires unwed mothers looking for public assistance to approach the father first. No more popping out babies and jumping on the dole. Dads, in this case, my cousin Archie, now have got to step up. But first, the mother must establish paternity.

Archie said he wasn't the father; Suellen said he was. The state did the DNA test. Then, as Maury might have said, "You are the father!" All of a sudden, Archie had twin toddlers. He came from a family that favored boys, with my Aunt April as matriarch. He was the second of four boys; all their names started with "A." It should have been A-okay.

But Kito was awkward, "non-verbal," perhaps even autistic—he was too young to test. His name started with a "K." The family was superstitious about stuff like that along with anybody who might be seen as "odd." Kito was odd and inconvenient. Besides, Archie already had a live-in girlfriend and their eight-month-old son, plus her one-year-old daughter (by a different father), and his seven-year-old son (by a different mother).

One day, Kito's mother dropped him off along with his twin sister at Archie's duplex and left town for an indeterminate time. She frequently littered the town with her children much as Archie did with his seed. The addition of the twins had the already cramped two-bedroom public housing unit overstretched like a balloon.

***

My younger sister, the Atlanta corporate executive who is a *Real Housewives* and *Maury* fan, called me during her lunch hour. We were three states apart, and I was sitting on my sofa in Houston, grading papers, having a San Francisco Symphony mug of Darjeeling nearby.

"Hey," ReeRee barked in the speed-of-light CEO voice. She's been the same since childhood; our parents called her "Chief" because of her bossiness. "Have you heard that one of Archie's sons disappeared? I just heard it from Isaac."

"Archie who?" I sputtered, unprepared for the onslaught. "Aunt April's son? Our cousin?"

"What are you talking about?"

"Archie has a son with one of his baby mamas. He was taking a nap when he was supposed to be taking care of the child. When he woke up, the child was missing."

"Oh my God! Where was the child's mother? Was she in the house?"

"No, the woman he was living with wasn't the child's mother, though I think he has a baby with her, too, or was that… Anyway, the woman was giving the other twin a bath or giving her own child a bath or something, and Archie was taking a nap. I think there were other kids in the house, as well."

"What the. . .? Well then, what happened?"

"It's on the news; I'm sending you a link."

***

The Disappearance

On Thursday, November 23, a 911 call came into police headquarters in Polydora, Oklahoma.

Neighbor: My neighbor's son is missing. He's two and a half years old.

Operator: Okay, and what is your name, ma'am?

Neighbor: Cindy Roberts.

Operator: Cindy?

Neighbor: Yes, ma'am.

Operator: R-O-B-E-R-T-S?

Neighbor: Yes, ma'am.

Operator: And how old's this little boy? Two years old?

Neighbor: Two and a half.

Operator: Two-and-a-half-year-old little boy?

Neighbor: Yes. It's been about 45 minutes.

Operator: What's he wearing?

Neighbor: (aside) Do y'all know what he's wearing? (pause) They think he was wearing blue shorts and a red-and-white striped shirt.

Operator: Okay. What's the address?

Neighbor: The address is 111 Beech Street. It's a block off 78.

Operator: Okay, ma'am. I'll send an officer right over there to you.

***

The First Story: He Must Have Walked Out of the House

Archie Albertson

Archie had been a high school sports star. With his 6'11" height advantage and natural ability, he dribbled and dunked his way to prime college offers, starring for two seasons as a Division I player at West Central Oklahoma State. According to the book *Best of Oklahoma Sports*, "Like Samson, he strong-armed the program atop his shoulders and heave-hoed it to a win against the University of Oklahoma." Despite his short tenure there, the Oilies inducted him into their Hall of Fame five years ago.

His academic talents were much less stellar, which is why the state's premier team hadn't rushed to recruit him in the first place. So, after five years in college, when he couldn't complete a degree, he dropped out and went off to play professionally with the Enid Tornados of the short-lived U.S. Basketball Federation, and then he played with a Uruguayan team in the International Basketball Federation. But his fear-based close-mindedness wouldn't allow him to eat food his mama hadn't made, even though foods like cuzcuz and pollo campero are close cousins to grits and fried chicken.

I saw him play once in college. Both my parents were college players, as was my brother-in-law. We didn't think he'd go far. Even with the colossal combo of physical gifts and natural ability, he couldn't make it. He had no hustle, no team spirit, and frankly, no brains. He simply thought that standing there shooting three-pointers was enough. He couldn't be taught. No running, no passing, and no strategy could be drummed into him. Just big feet superglued to the floor.

No profession can ever be conquered that way. Shaq and Serena Williams both have natural talent, a strong work ethic, and the ability to use deep strategic gifts. Though his parents had dreams of glory, Archie just couldn't muster the necessary work ethic, so he came back home to Polydora and led an aimless life of conceiving kids and flirting on Facebook.

Archie inherited traditional beliefs from his father with certain convenient modifications. In his early forties, he remained allergic to marriage. Though he wasn't supporting any of his kids or their mothers, he still believed that women should take care of all the "womanly" things like cooking, cleaning, and full-time childcare. After all, his mother had done the same. His mother, my college-educated aunt, did everything inside the house, but she also worked full-time as a chemistry teacher to support the family. But no, Archie's wasn't a single-parent home—technically.

Archie's father accepted his wife's labors, bringing little of himself to the family coffers, but fathering four big, strong boys. With virtually no education or skills, he did nothing more than occasional janitorial work.

Then there was that back injury. Pops said there was one; Worker's Comp said there wasn't. We'd never seen any indication of it as he played local basketball games out on the tarmac.

For twenty years after college, Archie lived the lay-about existence—hanging with his buds, smoking weed, and like his dad, working the occasional dead-end job. By age 43, he had eight kids by five different women. When this whole thing began, he was in public housing with a live-in girlfriend that his churchgoing mother called "trailer-trash" along with five kids of varying parentage: his, hers, mine, ours.

When Kito disappeared, volunteers fanned out week after week to search. News media publicized the search for months, avoiding the typical "here today, follow the bouncing ball tomorrow" pattern. Local sheriffs, state investigators, and FBI worked tirelessly to find the tiny boy. To no avail.

***

"The story's been on Nancy Grace!" ReeRee shouted over the phone. Well, maybe she wasn't shouting, but she has a naturally loud voice, and I was a bit dazed because I had been grading English Comp papers in complete silence for nearly two hours when the phone rang. Her information tazed me into full consciousness.

"What?!"

"She thinks there's something wrong with Archie's story."

"What did he say?"

"He says Kito must have just gotten out through the screen door while he was watching the other kids in the house."

"How many kids were there?"

"Who the hell knows. Both he and his girlfriend are in a yours-mine-and-ours situation."

I groaned "Oh lord" under my breath.

"Nancy Grace isn't buying it," my sister added breathlessly.

"Okay, what did *she* say?"

"She sent some of her staff to the house. She doesn't see how a child that young and that short could have opened that screen door. She thinks something doesn't smell right."

"You know, I've been thinking," I mused. "How was Archie sleeping when he had young children in the house? He might have fallen asleep and rolled over on the kid. As big as he is and as small as the child is, the child could have suffocated. It could happen."

"But then, where is the child?"

"I don't know. Good lord."

***

The Second Story: Somebody Must Have Snatched Him

April Albertson

My aunt, Archie's mother, is not much older than I. She's the youngest of thirteen from a rural share-cropping family. My father is the eldest. I'm *his* eldest. She was six-months old when he married, four years old when I was born.

Down in Polydora, Dad's family was known for their intelligence and their looks. They were the pride of the Black community, serving proudly in the military, teaching in schools, acting as deacons in the church.

April got the one trait but not the other. Her brains led to the college degree, the middle school science teacher job, and the high school chemistry job later. Looks-wise, she got the leftover features—her mother's large nose, her father's small eyes. But she's tall and stately, with a Jheri curl knockoff. Her formerly sharp mind has rusted from underuse and over-dependence on churchy small-mindedness. Somehow the good-natured confidence of her siblings morphed into judgmental arrogance. As years went by, we felt more and more isolated from her.

When April was a teenager, her mother died. My parents, living near D.C., agreed to take her in. ReeRee and I had been so excited for her to live with us, but she wanted to stay with her elderly father. For the first time in her life, she would be the total focus of her father's attention.

One summer, though, she spent time with siblings in Detroit and came back with Big Al, an illiterate guy she married. He barely spoke, rarely worked, but he thought he was cute and walked with a "playa's swagger." Big Al expected his wife to do all the traditional wifely things: cook, clean, conceive, while also bringing home the bacon from her teaching job. She bore him four boys, all of whom were named with the letter "A" after their parents.

April was the brains in her nuclear (in the quasi-bombing sense) family. All the boys, including her husband, depended on her judgment. She spoke with them; she spoke for them. But she always affected a quasi-convincing semblance of deference to her husband as the titular head (in the quasi-biblical sense) of the household.

Corporal punishment was the only way Al knew. Like many rural environments, it was an accepted way of life, culled from the Bible's orchard during scriptural cherry-picking season. "Spare the rod" made it to the processing plant, while "suffer the little children to come unto me" was left to rot on the tree.

Growing up, we knew April as being cheerful, but since marrying Al, she didn't seem happy. We rarely saw her big face-splitting smile.

Her boys grew up strong and tall like her. Physically. But they were all too work-averse and education-averse like their father. Since Archie, the favorite, failed at basketball, Lil' Al, the one who works for the postal service, is considered to be the success story.

None of them completed college, though two attended. But all lived up to "be fruitful and multiply" like their father. From four sons, April has twenty-four grandkids. Only one son has ever married (the steady-working one), and even he has children out of wedlock. All have multiple "baby mamas." Churchgoing April blames the bad girls for seducing her good boys, but none of her sons has ever lived with all his kids at any one time. And that's what pissed us off.

When Archie left the U.S. to play ball in Uruguay, he left all his children behind even though some were not living with their mothers. In our family history of hard work, military service, college degrees, good jobs, and good kids, April's is the anti-success story, conspicuous in its unfortunate consistency. The longer she lived with Big Al, the more judgmental she became.

***

"The whole area has turned out to look for him," ReeRee blared. "They've brought in helicopters and sniffer dogs, and a bunch of people volunteered to look for Kito."

"And they haven't found anything? Where could a child that young go?"

"Maybe he was snatched. Archie mentioned a white van to the po-po, but he was a repairman vouched for by the neighbor who had hired him."

"Oh my God. Oh my God. What does Nancy Grace say?"

"I think she's on to something. She still says there's something wrong with this picture, that the police should look at the family."

"What does April say?"

"She says she asked Archie over and over again if he knew anything and he keeps saying 'no'. She says she believes him."

"Hmmm. But why would she keep asking him if she believes him so much? She must think he's lying. And if she thinks so, he probably is. What on earth has he done?"

"I think you're right. You know he never could admit when he did something wrong. Remember when he stole those cookies April had made for Cousin Jo-Jo after she got out of the hospital?"

"He was only seven."

"But still, it just goes to show. I wonder where that baby is."

"Damn."

Y Kendall

The Third Story: Something Smells

Jerald "Big Al" Albertson, Sr.

He wears dapper clothes of synthetic colors, always topped with a Kangol cap rakishly tilted to the side. His dress is at odds with long-missing teeth. Ask him a question about politics, or the weather, or his missing grandson, and he'll just grunt and shrug, or say "I'ont know," or "Ask April." But mention dinner and he's likely to trample his grandchildren on his way to the kitchen. There he'll pile his plate high as Everest with food, not caring in the least whether enough is left for anyone else.

In fact, part of the family lore is when he did just that at a funeral meal and one of his smallest grandchildren began to cry because, after the adult men swarmed the table, there was no fried chicken left. Not even a wing. His son, Archie, moved toward the child with his hand reared back, ready to strike, but other relatives intervened. Cheryl, a social worker, calmed him down while Jake, my brother-in-law, whisked the child away.

Big Al looked all lost and confused when ReeRee asked why he didn't leave some food for the children. "But…" he mumbled, "I like my chicken hot."

***

"The search is still ongoing," my sister reported three months later. "The Missing Children people are there. Did you see the video link I sent you where Archie's hoping his son is returned? He's done the same in church"

"Well, at least he's going to church. But after all these months, where could that baby be?

I just hope he's not being abused. Jesus wept."

"No. Andy knows something. Remember when Momma and I went down there? She says Andy knows something. You know how she could always read boys after all her years of teaching."

"Which one is Andy? Al junior is the oldest, right?"

134

"Yeah. I think Andy is the one right after Archie. Who does that leave?"

"Uhhh, Allen?"

"That's right," she responded. "He's the youngest, I think. Al, Archie, Andy, Allen."

"All these A-names confuse the hell out of me."

"They've all got baby mamas."

"Are you kidding me?" I said, my voice filled with amazement. "Do they support them? I thought one of them was married."

"April takes care of some of Archie's. The one you're thinking of is Al Junior, the oldest one. He's the only one who has most of his kids living with him. But he's divorced and engaged, engaged to someone with an A-name . . . Annie, Andie, Andes, I don't know."

"Well, I guess that's something. Wait, Andes like the mountain range?"

"You know it can't be spelled like that," she chuckled. "That would be too much like something that makes sense."

"My people, my people," I moaned, wryly shaking my head. "All right then. Later."

***

Nobody seemed to know what happened. First, Archie said, "Maybe the screen door was open." Then, maybe he'd been kidnapped. Neighbors were questioned. Family members were questioned. Repair people with business vans were questioned. The full forces of state and federal law enforcement pulled out all the stops. Nobody seemed to know where Kito was.

Uncle Isaac, the family griot, reported more than once that Archie stood up in the church and begged people to pray for the safe return of his son. Kito's mother, Suellen, sobbed on camera, both local and national. Kito's twin sister, Alissa, kept piping, "Where Kiki? Where Ki-ki?" Archie's mother, April, fiercely blamed Kito's mother, Suellen. She told everyone who'd listen that Suellen used the baby to ruin Archie's life. Big

Y Kendall

Al speaks so little that the police couldn't even interview him for the entire year that his grandchild was missing.

Months came and months went. I taught my classes, my sister did her good works. No sign of Kito. But his twin kept asking for her Ki-ki.

Then, shortly after the spring flowers began to bud, the body was found. Tossed away like trash, covered in brush. Under closer questioning, Archie's stories fell apart. One of Kito's half-siblings opened up about past abuses. Archie had hit the unwanted toddler—often. That wasn't unusual in rural Oklahoma. "Spare the rod and spoil the child" and all that. But with such a big guy as Archie and such a small guy as Kito—an unwanted child at that—something was destined to go wrong.

***

"Oh my God! Archie's been arrested!"

"Whaaat! What has he done?"

"Andy admitted loaning Archie his van, but thought he was just taking the kids out for a picnic. With that clue, the sniffer dogs got on the scent."

"Even after all this time?"

"Yep. Apparently, Andy felt funny about using the van after the 'picnic,' so he just parked it. He's working steady now, so he bought an old banger."

"Forget the cars. What happened with Archie?"

"He fell apart and told the Feds he panicked."

"Panicked for a year? Panicked so much he could plead on TV? Panicked so much he could stand up in church and tell a bold-faced lie?" I got almost as loud as ReeRee.

"I've got the tapes of the interviews. One of the children innocently told about past 'whuppings' against Kito. Imagine how that child feels. It's horrible, just horrible."

Consequences

Big Al sustained his customary silence, even during the period when his son was charged with capital murder. When she came to the jail to check on her son after his arrest and heard about the charge, April wailed and fell out on the floor like Miss Rebecca used to do in church sometimes. Big Al stood there silent, unmoving, as his third son, Andy, rushed to pick up his mother from the dingy jailhouse linoleum.

ReeRee and I went down there to visit Archie in jail, surrounded by families and kids playing as they waited to visit other inmates. We'd never been in a jail before. Although she's a lawyer for a humanitarian non-profit, my sister is sharper than the jackleg lawyer they had gotten —and she was free.

The best capital murder lawyers in Oklahoma are white and expensive, but even had they had the money, Archie's family wasn't comfortable with White people, so they'd got a Black pastor with some sort of degree from some unaccredited law school somewhere. I'm not even sure he'd passed the bar. He had never tried so much as a shoplifting case. Because our cousin was guilty, ReeRee suggested that special plea—you know the one—the Alford plea (I thought of *Mad Magazine*), where you take punishment without admitting guilt, kind of like corporations who cheat or poison thousands, then pay out millions without officially taking responsibility. I think it worked for her former corporation, but like many things in families, better to keep that thought to myself.

"That plea might work," ReeRee told them. And it did. The court accepted the Alford plea, and Archie wouldn't get the death penalty. He would spend years in prison where we were sure he'd become a favorite with guards and prisoners alike. Usually child-killers are targets, but everybody knew his history as a high school and college b-ball star. And he'd played pro-ball; that saved him from the abuse most child-killers normally suffer. They could pretend to believe him when he said it was an accident.

Oddly, Archie likes prison because being in there relieves him of all responsibility. No job required. No childcare required. No squabbling women. Just hanging with the guys, enjoying tales of the glory days. Same as he used to do. He's living his best life.

But his mother, April, is having trouble sleeping at night and holding her head high in church.

And Kito's tiny twin sister still wonders where her Ki-ki is.

Titan Arum

Elina Kumra

Elina Kumra

y mother is a corpse flower. She reeks of decay. Day by day it collects in me—the heady scent of spoilage—until I'm fetid with it. The corm is buried in the soil of my heart, its swollen stem base soaking up each sweeping cruelty. For the longest time, I've found that stench intoxicating. I've even come to depend upon it—unable to imagine a life beyond its reach.

Today, the South African sun blazes long into the late afternoon. Out in the backyard, at home among the towering weeds, Mama roots for her pack of Black & Mild, then digs into it for the last cigarette, hidden under a flap of silver foil. Cross-legged on a square of jute, she strikes a match and holds the flaming head to her cigarette. Taking a long drag, she narrows her eyes and turns to look at me as the shredded tobacco flares blood-orange.

It's a withering look—her specialty. Under its glare, for seventeen years of my life, every last hope I've clung to has been scoured away. Each time I thought my spirits couldn't deflate any further, she found a way to exert more pressure. Like the wheels of our trailer, sunken deep in the rusty mud, I had more caving in to do.

"Why don't you just wander off and die? I fail to see what's keeping you here."

There's a strange blandness to her cutting remarks, despite their shocking nature. Like all her other flippant barbarities, they hang in the air between us, an article of malice, emblematic of Mama's inexhaustible supply. No answer is expected from me, let alone a protest. I know better than to take issue with her scorn. All that does is excite it further. Instead, I retreat into silence, which I imagine as a small box-like space, as much as I can presently lay claim to. My meager silence is not even a reproach, although Mama treats it as such—as if I were seeking to cast it over her, to smother her latest, rancid attack.

"You think that works on me?" she sneers. "The silent treatment?"

When I fail to reply, she grabs my wrist and twists its bony ridges until a mottled stretch of forearm is turned upward. Then she brands my flesh with her cigarette— adding a thirty-third black star. Together they dot my skin like a constellation of birthmarks. When the first dark mark seared my skin, I looked upon it with revulsion. Now, I endow these scars with untold meaning and locate redemption within them. Beneath their sprouting shadows, I sense my future pulsing, making for the light.

One winter afternoon, the sun wheeled around the room. I held my scarred forearm up and tilted it as if turning a globe, teasing the sun's flare while surveying the blasted territories. Pop! Pop! Pop! They'd nova—one by one—like a string of firecrackers. The act—the budding eternity of it—threw me into such a different space that, for all practical purposes, I was already dead.

I no longer ask myself why this is happening—the endless cycle of abuse. I quit trying after the eighteenth black star singed my flesh in December of last year. That scar, in concert with the others, struck me as a binding promise. The longer I looked at it, the more it suggested a singularity in the making. A wormhole that bridged to the future. The question of '*Why*?' disappeared into the horizon I saw there. I fed it to the silence and felt its gravity grow around me, expanding my zone of protection inch by inch.

I know there will come a day when it swallows me whole.

***

For decades, Mama battled mental illness. It frustrated everyone's best efforts to cure her—family, friends, priests, seers, palmists, crystal healers, and holy fools alike. Her temples were rubbed with eucalyptus balm, steamed with herbal infusions. They girded her with garnet amulets to ward off evil and adorned her fingers with auspicious stones. All to no effect. Nothing lifted the wretched burden. Neither blistering mustard poultices nor pleading prayers could put an end to her ravings. She would wake in the dead of night, energized by grisly dreams, compelled to reenact them. Instead of fleeing their clutches, Mama gave the terrors a constant voice.

Finally, her father took her to the nearest polyclinic, where she was subjected to a battery of tests that proved no more effective than folk medicine. The exasperated doctor, conceding defeat, suggested marriage as a palliative. Maybe a husband could keep the worst of her madness in check, even if he lacked the wherewithal to root it out.

Her father placed a one-line advertisement in the village newspaper to solicit a groom: 'GIRL, EDO TRIBE, DARK-SKINNED, HEIGHT 140 CENTIMETRES, SEEKS HUSBAND.'

For months no one responded. Meanwhile, Mama jumped ahead on her matrimonial duties. One morning her mother found her lying on a coir cot, turned away from the pile of sick she had heaved up in the night. Her distended belly, no longer bound with muslin wraps, confirmed the source of the nausea. She would never reveal the man's identity, or even admit to sexual congress, but there was no doubting the end result.

Now that Mama's star had dimmed again, her father was forced to sweeten the original offer. The word 'DOWRY' was added to the text, widening the net of potential spouses to include the nakedly opportunistic. Who else—under the circumstances—would accept such damaged goods?

The groom fled before I was born—seduced a white woman in Lagos and left before my mother could curse his fleeing footsteps. He took with him the gems she'd kept wrapped in a clamshell purse, the last assets still to be gambled away as if awarding himself another dowry to burn through.

Estranged from the rest of her family, Mama found employment as a stairwell sweeper, sleeping at the base of a rundown apartment building on the outskirts of Dar es Salaam, known as "Death's District." There, she curled on newsprint bedding, her quilt riddled with mites. Every morning, she shook it out at the adjacent alley as the crows feasted on vegetable peel flung from the kitchens of the next-door restaurant. Then, with a bucket and reed broom braced under one arm, she began to dispense her lowly duties: hobbling up and down the stairwells, sweeping all before her, even as the pain chewed through her arthritic left knee.

By 9 a.m., perspiration had already left black moons beneath her armpits. Not that she lost herself in these exhaustive tasks. It was a way of reclaiming her bitter grievances, keeping them on a constant simmer. Under her breath—or, just as often, above it—Mama enumerated her countless indignities, pausing only to readjust the skeleton keys tied to her sari; her mawkish soliloquies, riddled with maudlin sentiments, echoing from floor to floor.

In time, the building got upgrades, with porcelain sinks installed in each apartment. The workmen hammered, shouted, spat, and cursed as they worked. By then, Mama was used to the building's residents looking through her as if she no longer existed. Still, it came as a shock when these day laborers followed suit in failing to offer her the slightest acknowledgment, though she occupied the building night and day.

On the final day of her employment, Mama wandered up to the roof, resting where the light spilled into the stairwell. There, she set her lunch to boil on her bucket of coals and monitored the flame with a plaited palm fan. While cooking egusi soup, she felt something tugging on the free end of her sari. When she looked down, her skeleton keys had vanished, and the dregs of her life savings with them. She raced down the stairs, retracing her steps, knocking over the coal bucket snagged to her sari, setting the building on fire.

***

Mama placed a premium on love in marrying my father—staking everything on that brittle idea. Little wonder that a smoldering hatred replaced it in the wake of her abandonment, growing ever more intense and all-encompassing. It was inevitable, then, that her hatred would encompass me too. I became the avatar of her failures. Born six months after the dissolution of her marriage, I symbolized all of its enduring humiliations. It's only a wonder she didn't pack me off to the nearest orphanage. Although, by then she was addicted to these raging sorrows—

forever raking over the coals of the past—and I could always help her in this all-important respect.

My child. That's what she called me. It's the first form of address I can remember, along with the damning intonation. I was doused in sarcasm from the very beginning. She made it sound like an accusation, as if I wasn't her child, but only professed as such. When I heard other mothers use the same two words, it shocked me—the difference in register. They poured their hearts into them, conjuring a powerful endearment. My mother would smother the words with vitriol until they amounted to a slap in the face.

It was the same with the rest of her lexicon. Language served one function—to denigrate the whole of existence. While other parents taught their daughters the alphabet with songs and goofy faces, I was treated to scowls and damning indictments: bitch, baggage, burden.

I learned which words to look out for. The most faithful precursors to violence. It's how I became a shrinking child, just shy of a vanishing act, always ready to disappear from view.

At the tail end of spring, the burn marks number 43 and the silence resulting from them is expansive, almost sensual. I reside at my silence's center, breathing it in—a rich, loamy odor that keeps the corpse flower at bay and buffers her many cruelties. Mama can sense it too, my growing imperviousness, which is why her anger flares more regularly. She can sense her powers waning. She has never been more impotent, despite her redoubled efforts. Every time she ramps up her sadism, my silence rises to meet the challenge.

Her wrath, for all its terrible stamina, is on the verge of bleeding out.

By April's end, she takes to burning my flesh every other day. The molten stars coalesce, forming a single jagged outline. It doesn't look like a black hole, but that's how I think of it—a great devourer. Everything within its orbit is destined to be absorbed; nullified. I don't know what it augurs exactly, but I'm thrilled by its enveloping presence. Inside its ever-darkening folds, I've learned to smoke my fears out.

On the first Thursday in May, as I study my forearm in bed, Mama bursts into my room unannounced and stares at me triumphantly.

"I knew it!" she says. "You've started worshipping them! You think they're a mark of distinction."

I look at her, arm still raised, feeling nothing—yet that nothingness has a fertile quality. It's the opposite of deadened. Something wild will grow from the depths of it. All I need to do is honor it first. Let it absorb the last of Mama's ire.

"Let me tell you something—you are a black dot," she thunders. "Don't ever forget that. Your life is a stain on the records."

My heart beats steady as I hear her out. She can no longer whip it into a frenzy. It feels like an enchantment, that slow, unchecked rhythm of mine.

Mama takes three steps forward, halving the distance between us. "Have you ever asked yourself why I punish you so?"

"Yes. Once. Not now."

She balks at the reply. The whites of her eyes flash. Her worst fears have been realized. I decline to play along. I watch this dawn on her—my resignation from our decades-long drama. Her mouth hangs open to search for a savage barb that will return me to my former station, but nothing can drag me back. At a loss, she rushes over to the wardrobe in the corner and seizes my few possessions, tossing them into the canvas bag hanging on the back of the door.

I see the logic at once. I have exhausted my use for her. This has been true ever since I stopped trying to make sense of Mama's actions. Unless I continue to wrestle with my anguish, she is ready to show me the door.

"I want you gone from here," she says, throwing the bag at the foot of the bed. "You're old enough to fend for yourself. It's long past time you started."

It's the only card she has left to play, yet I barely register it. I simply turn back the bedsheet, rise from the mattress, and start to dress.

"You have nowhere to go," she says.

I smile. I can't help myself. The way she says nowhere makes it sound like everywhere. Mama has lost her hold on language as well.

After dressing, I collect the bag and place it over my shoulder. I owe it to the silence to say nothing more. It's what divides us. I need to keep it that way—upholding the separation. No parting words for Mama to feast on or dissect in the coming months.

Some people have mothers, I have a Titan arum. I walk past the full skirt of her spathe, through the front room, and turn the handle on the door. Then I'm outside in the humid darkness, cutting through the tall weeds, heading for the gate that borders the back roads. The night is clear, and a three-quarter moon hangs high in the firmament. I open the gate and close it behind me, joining with Mother Night.

Babe in Arms

(poetry collection)

Monique Franz

Monique Franz

Babe in Arms

Inspired by "Baby in the Aftermath," a photo captured by H. S. Wong (Chinese 1900-1981) during the Second Sino-Japanese War. The subject, an infant left alone in the ruins of a bombed Shanghai South railway station during World War II (August 28, 1937).

At the end of your celebratory cigar
are the ashes of a mother's hold—
the lashes of her sudden absence.

Sitting in your victory is her orphaned hope,
wailing for the comfort
of those soft breasts,
now blown to bits.

And you sleep well
as the baby wears the dirt of your deeds
on their smudged, innocent cheeks;
cheeks the mother rubbed against her own,
savoring
her expectation of a future.

You feel no shame,
one so far removed from the territory
that you had to control.

You gave orders to one
who gave orders to one
who barked them into
the ears of another child—
this one uniformed,
not much older than this.
Expendable, he was.

"Bomb the station," you said,
without regard for its contained souls,
its vulnerable life,
the unexpectant flesh and blood.

You cowards of power,
you saw no timber fall,
you heard no seismic boom;
you felt no heat,
you smelled no char.

Yet, this baby was born
to bear all of your undoing—
your soulless doing,
for you to feel man enough
to square your suit
in a room full of
other godless fools
of which the daggers of hell await.

Monique Franz

No Applause

*Inspired by the art piece "Winter Moonlight" by American artist,
Charles Ephraim Burch (1893-1967).*

He details my winter
in ink, pencil, and crayon:
trees, meant for shelter,
give instead

        barrenness
   and

sharp edges.

Trees, hoped for seed,
stand stingily with no applause,

     a different kind of
          shade.

Moonlight,
ordained to emit vision, simply

                  glares.

An eye of ridicule
and portal of

          skepticism.

The judgmental eye is so bright though,
that it lit the whole

              damned

                    forest.

      Now, I see—if nothing else—
where the thorns are.

            And I still run,

                        unfazed,

            knowing just where

the spikes lie.

Monique Franz

Clipped Wings

The cage is open,
her neck—unbound.
The captors are gone,
 blinders removed.
And now—
 what does she do
 without someone to force her?

Where does she fly
with clipped wings?

She has no more tormentors—
except the bully within,
who taunts, "Fly, you stupid bird."
She thinks,
 I no longer want to fly.

"In the cage,
I longed to soar
until it ached.
And I sang
the songs of my pain."

Many admired the bird's songs,
and others
plucked her feathers.
She didn't mind—
as long as admiration was there.

But none would stay after they plucked,
and so her pain was great.

Very few feathers
remained,
and part of her wanted
the others gone too.

She wasn't sure if this was
out of love,
or solely
out of fear—
just so there'd be
no more feathers to take.

And now?
Where does she go?
Does she dare believe—
with clipped wings
and far less feathers—
that she has any worth
outside of the cage?

Est. 1991

(poetry collection)

Najib Abbi

Najib Abbi

Geeljire

When he fell to the floor,

I told him "Stand up,

We need to run!"

He said he never learned to run,

Only to walk and whistle alongside camel.

He said he's never tasted blood,

Only black tea with sugar.

He's never carried a rifle,

Only a cane on his back.

He never learned to duck

or count bullets,

Only to prostrate

and count blessings.

He never met any enemies,

Only family.

His tongue never learned to scream,

Only to speak in poetry.

He's never needed to be a soldier,

Only a camel herder.

He's never known war,

Only nabad

Earthquake

The earth shattered,

like it was nothing,

like its solidity was but a mirage,

a vacant promise,

an illusion to keep us all in check.

The earth shattered,

like it was a frail piece of glass,

every inch that it cracked, another mile of disappointment,

and every lesson that it taught me

lost its merit.

The ground withered,

like the dead didn't depend on it to rest,

and the trees didn't plant their roots there,

like every ant from every colony didn't reside beneath it.

The earth shattered,

It wasn't ever meant to,

but the earth shattered,

and with it our hopes and dreams.

The earth shattered,

and we had to hold it all together.

Najib Abbi

Too Much, Not Enough

Can't you see it on my face,
Can't you see the chips in my nails,
And the dirt in my hair,
Can't you tell that I just climbed out of a tomb,
That I've been alone,
And out of the sun's reach,
My only company the worms,
But they didn't want my flesh,
They said it was too warm,
And the parasites,
But they didn't want me as a host,
They said I was too broken,
And the roots,
But they didn't want to be near me,
They said I was too hollow,
And the dead,
But they didn't want my conversation,
They said I knew nothing,
And then I came here,
And they said I was too used,
Too fractured, too tormented,
Too charred to walk amongst the living

Too depressed to smile back politely,
Too tortured African to be patriot American,
My name too ethnic,
My home too war torn,
Our sun too hot,
My people's throats too dry,
And their stomachs too empty,
Nothing easy on the eyes,
Too much pain to just let get by,
Then they said I didn't come from enough,
Not nearly enough for an even trade,
I didn't come from enough sympathy,
Or enough rain, not enough food,
Not enough laughter, or shining smiles,

Not enough space in the cemetery,
Our graves are suffocating,
Not enough room in the masjid,
Everyone wants to speak to God,
Not enough answers for all their questions,
Not enough tears being caught,
Or grass growing where they drop,
Not enough dreams, not enough bandages for
bleeds,
not even enough sleep,
Not enough, not enough, not enough

A person only flees home when it's not enough,
or when it's just too much,
And in turn is too much, and just not enough.

Najib Abbi

A Different World

In a different world,

I can remember the face,

the voice,

and the poetry of my great-grandfather,

there's enough rice for everyone,

and my mother yells at me for trailing sand home from the beach

In a different world,

my siblings and I inherit the rivers our father told us of in legend,

and we swim with our cousins,

as he once swam with his,

In a different world,

I roam the same streets my mother used to as a child,

and our neighbors say I'm almost as troublesome as she was,

and we laugh

In a different world,

all our children speak their language,

we never need for anything or anyone outside our walls,

we don't trudge through deserts or get lost at sea seeking asylum,

nobody *loses* their life trying to *find* refuge,

and we don't ever miss home anymore

In a different world,

we have home.

The Dream Blocker

Michelle Oxford

Michelle Oxford

Usually, I'd pinch myself to make sure I wasn't dreaming, but the sharp pain in my elbow from hitting it against the 'Ife Head' assured me this moment was real. Tonight, I'd bring the vibrant artistry of Osogbo, Nigeria to the bustling heart of Chicago. After what I had been through, it was hard to believe this was happening. Nursing my arm, I moved through the gallery, directing workers. Everything had to be perfect.

"Olumide," I called. My eyes located my assistant among the workers unloading the truck. "Make sure that piece is handled with care. It's the centerpiece of this exhibition."

Olumide nodded. His brown skin glistened with sweat from the heat outside. "I got you, Nandi. Don't worry."

"That Nok-style terracotta head must be placed by the entrance. It needs to make a statement as soon as people walk in," I instructed, pointing.

Olumide approached me, the artwork towering over his short stature. I smiled at the sight. "Where do you want it?" he asked, struggling to see from behind the painting.

"Centerstage. It's going to be the focal point."

He nodded and carefully positioned the painting so that it was no longer overpowering him.

The painting did something to my mood, and I stood silent, staring at it.

"What's on your mind, Nandi?"

"I'm just remembering some things."

Olumide removed his glasses and stepped closer as if he could see better without them. His eyes traced the artwork. "It's breathtaking," he murmured.

The painting was a large canvas dominated by a solitary, glistening needle caught mid-fall against a backdrop of muted, earthy tones. The needle, detailed with intricate patterns and faint etchings of Yoruba symbols, seemed almost alive, suspended in the air as if time had frozen.

I took a deep breath, my voice barely above a whisper as I explained, "I call it the Needle. It's more than just a painting to me. It represents the Yoruba proverb— 'bí abẹ́rẹ́ bo lọwọ adẹ́tẹ̀, yóò dẹ́tẹ̀'—a needle that falls off a leper's hand…"

"…can never be retrieved. I love that saying," Olumide added.

I looked around the gallery, a mix of emotions playing through me. My mind drifted back to a year ago after I received the email that gave life to my dream.

***

I had felt a surge of excitement and pure triumph after seeing the words, "We are pleased to invite you…" Weeks later, as I stood there searching for my car keys, those initial feelings were overshadowed by a lingering fear.

The muscles in my neck tightened as I inhaled sharply, trying to steady myself. My palms started to sweat as my body entered fear mode. "No," I told myself, "Not today."

There was no way I could miss this event—a launching pad for upcoming artists like me to showcase our work. It was a small, intimate gathering with five specially invited African artists.

I had prepared thoroughly, spending weeks perfecting my pieces, rehearsing their storylines, and choosing the perfect outfit. My collection was polished, and my contemporary Nigerian style was impeccable. While this was my first charity show in the United States, I had already participated in similar events back home, one of them for a hospital. That was where I met Justin.

Justin. When we met, I had thought that compared to the other guys I dated, Justin was more dependable, more together, more... everything. Everyone thought I had hit the jackpot—a young, polite, handsome Black doctor. We got married, and I migrated to the United States. He was always there to catch me when I stumbled while learning the ways of his country. Now, I realized Justin had a brooding, controlling nature. He was possessive, monitoring my every move and questioning me under the guise of caring. After five years, he had managed to isolate me from friends and family.

Michelle Oxford

The day before the charity show, he claimed his car was in the shop and had used mine. Now, I needed the car to go, and the keys were nowhere to be found. Could this be another one of his tricks to keep me dependent on him?

I threw the couch cushions to the floor and ran my fingers along the gap. I paused to reposition my wedding band, which had shifted out of place. This was exactly why it mattered to vacuum everywhere, despite Justin calling it obsessive. No dust balls or sticky residue were on my hands.

But also, no keys.

I exhaled and walked to the kitchen. I rummaged through the bowl of miscellaneous items, pushing aside pens, paper clips, and old receipts. I checked under a pile of mail and even opened the junk drawer, sifting through its contents. I propped my hands on my hips, looking around the room. This exquisite room within the stunning house that Justin had provided seemed determined to do its master's will, trapping me along with my dreams.

"I'm going to be late. Where could they be?" I muttered to myself, panic setting in.

I picked up my phone and looked at Justin's number. I paused. If I called to ask him where the keys were, he would twist reality, making me doubt my memories and feelings. His pattern of gaslighting had become all too familiar. He'd make me feel incompetent for misplacing things I was sure I hadn't touched.

While he was always charming and sociable outside, at home, he was a different person. He criticized my every move, making me feel small and inadequate.

My phone rang, startling me. It was my mother-in-law.

"Hello?" I answered.

"Nandi, are you okay? You sound out of breath."

"I can't find my car keys and I'm running late," I explained, trying to keep the panic out of my voice.

"Oh dear, that's not good. Do you want me to come and take you? I can be there in ten minutes," she offered.

I hesitated. "That would be great. Thank you," I finally said, relief flooding my voice.

When my mother-in-law arrived, I checked my reflection in the hall mirror, trying to find myself. A middle-aged Nigerian woman dressed in a flowing Ankara dress stared back at me. Her smooth, dark skin glowed with a natural radiance, and her high cheekbones accentuated her striking features. Her large, expressive eyes held a depth of emotion, framed by long lashes and perfectly arched brows. Her full lips, glossed with a hint of color, curved slightly as she assessed her appearance.

I thought back on my journey with contemporary art. I had gone to school to master the blend of Western styles and traditional Nigerian techniques. This unique fusion had become the foundation of my work. Through years of dedication, I created pieces that resonated deeply, making me a standout artist back home and now hopefully in the United States.

I closed my eyes and vowed to never forget who I was.

I grabbed my things and hurried out the door. "Thank you so much for doing this, Mom," I said, climbing into the car.

"No problem at all, dear. I know how important this show is for you." She smiled warmly.

My mother-in-law, Mrs. Jenkins, was in her early sixties, having a welcoming presence that instantly put people at ease. Her ebony skin was smooth and radiant. She wore her silver-streaked, kinky-curled hair in its natural state. Her eyes had a way of making you feel seen.

"You're like the daughter I never had," she said, resting her arm on the back of my seat and looking over her shoulder as she backed out of the driveway. "Just know I'm always here for you. As an immigrant, I understand the struggles and the need for support."

I tried to relax. "I just don't understand where the keys could have disappeared to," I murmured, mostly to myself.

"Don't worry about it now. Just focus on the show. You've worked so hard for this."

Michelle Oxford

We arrived later than we wanted as there was traffic on the way. A large Maasai warrior statue stood at the entrance, welcoming us. Its presence was comforting. As I walked by, I felt goose bumps from its energy. My initial worry was now replaced by a sense of being home in Nigeria.

Inside, the rhythmic pounding of djembe drums instantly filled the air, each beat thumping in my chest.

Dancers glided gracefully in a circle, their vibrant kente cloths shimmering in the light. As we walked over to my display area, my heart filled with pride and thrill. This was my culture on display.

"Mom, do you see all those exquisite pieces!" I exclaimed, looking around at the other booths.

"Hush, child. Your work is beautiful, and I dare say much better," she replied, giving me a warm hug.

A familiar voice called out, "Nandi!"

I turned to see Justin walking toward my booth with a glass of Chapman in hand. For a split second, a flicker of surprise crossed his face. Despite his tall and skinny frame, he moved with surprising grace. His dark complexion contrasted sharply with the white dress shirt and grey blazer he wore. His eyes, inherited from his mother, carried a certain intensity, while his smile, though outwardly charming, had an underlying hint of menace.

"I'm so sorry I'm late. I had to perform an emergency surgery and couldn't get away," Justin explained, kissing his mother on the cheeks.

"It's okay," I replied, trying to keep my voice even. "We just got here."

A small sigh escaped his lips. "Let me guess. Keys missing again?" His attempt at playfulness fell flat as he continued, "I keep telling you, everything needs its place."

His casual remark about the keys struck me, and a sinking feeling settled in my stomach. They had always hung in their place before. His comments had a way of chipping away at the trust I had in myself, making me second-guess everything I did. I didn't need this right now.

"The food looks amazing. Have you tried the suya or the puff-puff yet?" Justin asked, his eyes scanning the table laden with various appetizers.

My spirit deflated. He had made no mention of my art pieces. "Not yet," I replied, turning to a passing waiter to ask for a glass of ginger beer.

As the evening wore on, Justin's grip on my arm would tighten whenever I engaged with someone for too long. He was polite and charismatic, but I could feel the underlying tension. I tried to focus on the positive comments from the attendees, soaking in the validation that my work deserved.

Toward the end of the event, an influential gallery owner approached my booth. "Your work is extraordinary," he said. "I would love for you to do a solo exhibition at my gallery."

My eyes widened with excitement. "Thank you so much! That would be a dream come true."

I rushed to tell the news to Justin and my mother-in-law, who were by the appetizer table.

"Justin, Mom, you won't believe it," I exclaimed, excitement bubbling over. "I have been offered a chance to do a solo exhibition! This could be my big break!"

Justin turned his attention back to the puff-puff and said dismissively, "That's wonderful, darling, but remember, you need to be practical. Art doesn't pay the bills."

My heart sank. I had hoped for just a tiny bit of support from him.

Mrs. Jenkins's eyes lit up with genuine delight. "Oh, that's fantastic news, dear! You've worked so hard for this. We should celebrate!"

Justin, ignoring his mother's enthusiasm, said abruptly, "Let's go. I have a headache."

"Already?" his mother responded. "I'll take her back when it's over."

"No, Mom, we are leaving now," he snapped, pulling me as he walked away. As we drove home, I stared out the window. The city lights blurred as tears welled in my eyes.

Justin's grip on the steering wheel tightened, his knuckles white.

"Who was that man you were talking to?" he demanded, breaking the silence.

I hesitated, knowing how quick-tempered he could be.

"Angelo," I replied softly. "He's the gallery owner who offered me the solo exhibition."

Justin scoffed. "I don't trust him. The way he was looking at you. You need to stay away from him."

My heart pounded. "Justin, he's a professional contact. This is my career we're talking about."

Justin's brows furrowed. "What career? You're not seeing him again."

The tears streamed down my face. "Justin, please. This is important to me. You can't control who I talk to."

Justin pulled the car over abruptly, turning to face me. "You listen to me, Nandi. I am your husband. I know what's best for you. You're not going to see him again," he said, grabbing me by the arm.

My mind raced. I felt trapped. Fear coursed through my veins as I struggled to breathe. I knew I had to play along—for now. "Okay, Justin. Okay!" I choked out, terrified of what he might do next.

Justin's expression softened slightly, but the tension remained. "Good. Now let's go home and forget about this… this hobby."

I nodded, my heart breaking.

Without warning, he slammed his foot on the gas pedal. "You just don't get it, do you?" he muttered.

The car lurched forward. I was jolted back in my seat. The engine roared as the speedometer needle climbed. My eyes widened in fear.

"Justin! What are you doing? Slow down!"

Justin's sight was fixed on the road ahead. He ignored my pleas, the car hurtling down the winding road at a reckless speed.

"Maybe this will show you how serious I am, Nandi. Maybe this will make you understand," he said.

I grabbed onto the dashboard.

"Justin, please! Slow down!"

"Maybe that's what it takes for you to listen!"

A sharp turn appeared ahead, and Justin barely slowed down. The car skidded, tires screeching as they fought for traction on the asphalt.

I screamed.

The car fishtailed, coming perilously close to the edge of the road where a steep drop loomed.

In a moment of clarity, Justin jerked the wheel, correcting its course just in time. The car straightened out. He finally eased off the gas, and the car slowed to a safer speed. I was breathing heavily. I looked at Justin with a mixture of fear and anger.

"What is wrong with you, Justin? You could have killed us!"

Justin glanced at me, his expression softening just slightly. For a moment, regret flickered in his eyes, but it was quickly replaced by a hardened resolve.

"I'm sorry. But you need to understand, Nandi. This is for your own good." I shook my head, wiping my cheeks with the back of my hand.

"Pull over, Justin. I want to get out."

Justin glanced at me. "You can't be serious."

"I am serious, Justin. Pull over!"

Justin hesitated, then swerved the car to the side of the road, the tires kicking up gravel as they came to a stop. The city was now behind us, and the road was flanked by dense woods on either side.

I unbuckled my seatbelt, my movements hurried and tense. I reached for the door handle. "Nandi, don't do this. You're overreacting."

I swung the door open, pulled up my dress, and stepped out onto the gravel shoulder. I turned back to face Justin.

"No, Justin. I'm done. I can't do this anymore."

Justin watched me for a moment, his expression a mix of anger and desperation. He slammed his hands on the steering wheel in frustration.

"Fine! Have it your way! Oh, and you might need these," he said, reaching into his jacket pocket.

Michelle Oxford

A flash of silver whirled through the air and landed with a sharp clink at my feet. Without waiting, Justin shifted the car back into drive and sped off with the door opened. I watched as the car disappeared down the road, leaving me standing alone in the dark.

I took a deep breath and looked around, the reality of my situation sinking in. The road stretched out in both directions, empty and silent. I pulled out my phone, but there was no signal. I started walking, my footsteps crunching on the gravel. I whispered a silent prayer to my Ori for strength and guidance. When I looked over my shoulder and saw the headlights of a car coming into view, my heart leaped. It was my mother-in-law's car.

Mrs. Jenkins pulled over quickly, the car stopping just ahead of me. She jumped out, worry etched across her face.

"Nandi! Are you okay?"

As I rushed toward her, tears stung my eyes. My shoulders slumped. I felt guilty for relying on her again that night and couldn't meet her eyes.

Mrs. Jenkins wrapped her arms around me, holding me tight. "I saw how Justin was behaving, so I followed him. But then he sped off back there." Mrs. Jenkins's eyes softened. "Nandi, how long has this been going on?"

I felt the tears well up. "For a while," I admitted. "I was too ashamed to tell anyone." Mrs. Jenkins's face tightened with resolve. "Nandi, if you want to leave, I will help you."

"Look what he had all this time!" I said, pulling the evidence from my pocket.

Her eyes widened in recognition. "Your car keys!"

A moment of silence hung between us before we both burst into laughter, the sound carrying into the stillness of the night.

Mrs. Jenkins shook her head. "Let's get off this lonely road," she said, looking around nervously. "Come and stay with me for a while."

As we walked to the car, my eyes filled with tears again.

Mrs. Jenkins started the car and said, "I'm sorry I didn't see it earlier.

You had no support system here, and I failed you. But don't worry. I've got you. We'll figure out something together. Who would have thought that my son was a dream blocker?"

***

"Nandi! Are you okay? Nandi!" Olumide's voice brought me back to the present.

I turned to him, offering a small smile. "I'm fine, just reflecting, Olumide."

He nodded understandingly. "I know just what we need," he said as he tapped into the playlist on his phone, and the rhythmic pulse of Afro beats filled the air.

"When did you get a chance to set up the speaker system?" I asked, surprised.

"Earlier," he said, his shoulders rolling in time with the beat.

Mrs. Jenkins approached us with a proud smile. "Are we partying or are we working?"

"Both," Olumide and I replied in unison, laughing at our synchronized timing.

"You've done it, Nandi," she said, her eyes shining with pride. "I'm so proud of you."

I hugged her tightly, a hint of playfulness in my voice as I said, "Hey, the day is not over yet. We still need to keep an eye out for you-know-who."

Crossing

Sufiya Abdur-Rahman

At first, I feared the water. So close, moving in ripples that seemed to stretch out like open arms just over the edge. I crossed the Chesapeake Bay Bridge on my way to work on Maryland's Eastern Shore, and my car felt too close to the water. My driving became a caress of the minuscule guardrail that I was sure could do nothing to stop a careening tractor-trailer or a mighty crosswind from throwing or blowing my sedan down into the waves. I was afraid of the deep—its cold, choppy expanse complicit in the capture and conveyance of my ancestors to this land and this very waterway's shores—so I grabbed the steering wheel with both hands. One at ten and one at two, like I'd been taught but never, until then, used. It didn't help.

If all the reverberations from those multi-ton hunks of metal on wheels, or a strike from another oversized barge below, managed to crumble the bridge, and mile-long sections descended into the Bay, what would it matter if I'd finally abandoned my tenuous single-handed hold? I'd be trapped, strapped in by that infernal safety belt, cascades pouring into my wind-whipped car from cracked-in-spring, fully-open-in-summer windows to drown me. No rescuer would reach me in time. Even if I somehow managed to unbuckle myself and escape the flooded car, either stereotype or cultural imperative dictates that I can't swim. Crossing this damn bridge to get to work will be the death of me, I thought as vehicles accelerated past me.

But the truth is: I have always been afraid of heights. As a little girl, I felt dizzy observing the New York City skyline from the nineteenth-floor terrace of my uncle's Bronx apartment and got lightheaded when my father brought me to the World Trade Center's 107th floor restaurant for my eighteenth birthday. I only took this job—knowing I'd have to cross the bridge—because I thought I would get used to it and be able to handle the discomfort. You know, conquer my fear. It wasn't working.

But then, I stopped looking down. Repeatedly, my gaze fell, because I was too fearful to lift my chin, square my shoulders, and face what lay before me.

At eye level, I had to confront the reality of my position: suspended in the heavens. As my car climbed the bridge's curve, heading east from home, my eyes could do nothing but ascend with it, seemingly toward the firmament. For a stretch, there was nothing up there. No skyscrapers, no bridge towers, cords, or cables: No toll booths or houses or people or roads. Only the occasional seagull amidst clouds, sun, sky, and the unmistakable presence of the Most High. Around and above me—my Creator conjured all I saw: golden sun rays piercing throug h billowy white puffs, the expanse of blue in every direction, the systems of rotation, gravity, and the unseen atmospheric gas that made it all possible.

So, what in God's name was I, in my little black four-door, doing there? I shouldn't be here. I shouldn't be here. I shouldn't be here. The words rang in my head, but they didn't come out of my mouth because I was holding my breath. I had two hands gripping the steering wheel, trying not to look up into the face of Allah or down into the bottomless lagoon, but straight ahead at the bumper of the car in front of me. I did this until I returned to solid ground—where I was rightfully in control, where I exhaled.

When up that high, coasting on my own power, my presence feels unearned. I want to be ready—to have accomplished enough, loved enough, been loved enough, and lived enough to feel ready to meet my Maker. But I wasn't. This, not the water, terrified me. My insignificance against such magnificence made me shudder. And so, I crossed the bridge. I got to work.

The next time my car began the climb and my eyes drifted skyward toward the firmament, awestruck by the wonders of the world, I chanted, "Subhan'Allah. Subhan'Allah," like a howling dervish marveling at, yet pleading for, Allah's protection.

I lowered the sun visor and kept driving forward.

Locked

Sonia Kinyua

The mantra my mother repeated as she mercilessly detangled my locs with the fresh bottle of *Just Me* before school every day. *Twist. Part. Twist. Part.*

My head jerked side to side while my mother slicked my hair into another ponytail. It was a style that all little Black girls knew; a style all little Black girls had—one this little Black girl hated. The pulling, tugging, brushing, combing. With each tug, I felt I lost a chunk of hair. The tightness of each braid, twist, and ponytail was never worth the kick-drumming in my head.

"Stop moving!" "Stop touching!" "Move your hand."

The phrases echoed in my mind. I cringed as her calloused fingers took another strand to braid my hair. Tears welled but dared not fall, for fear of another mantra. The pools grew, making each blink harder than the last. The only barrier between my mother's claws and the tears threatening to fall was the sleep that finally overtook me. My body numbed to the rhythm in my head—until the world faded into silence and darkness.

*****

Kicking my feet on the edge of the three-foot pool, I peer over at my friends swimming along the water, doing tricks and flips like synchronized swimmers. Lexi's long blonde hair trails behind her as she emerges from the sandy pool floor. Amber follows. As she comes up from the chlorinated water, her bangs stick to her sun-bathed skin. Behind her golden trail, my swim cap swells. I felt like a kid in those Airhead commercials. I retreated to a corner as my neon headcover, glowing like a sign, brought attention to my hidden locs.

The girls around me reminded me of Baywatch—their bikinis and golden locs flowing in the wind. All while I sat in my one-piece and cap, having the water lap around my wrinkled feet. My misery eased somewhat as I watched the fun, but I still felt overshadowed by the way their hair flowed through the water, shimmering in the sunlight as they came up. There were no golden locs following me, just a bright green swim cap, fastened tight around my head.

Finally, I ripped off my swim cap to let my twisted locs loose in the water. My mother's hard work was destroyed in this wave of defiance. As I glided into the pool, the twists waded in the chlorinated water. My confidence was soon diminished as I came up to the surface, seeing that my once-long locs had shrunken to meet the hairs on my chin.

"How did your hair get so short?"

I crouched back, peering into the reflection of Lexi's goggles as the water absorbed in my hair whispered insults into my ears. I shrunk in the way my long twists had. My friends descended upon my hair, invading, no, violating, my space, running their fingers in my now tangled wet locs. Suddenly, the spotlight was on me; stares intensified along with inquisitive glares as if none had ever seen such curls before.

Thereafter the others got over the fascination with my shriveled hair. As the sun set, my hair dried and tangled and we headed home.

I dreaded meeting my mother's wrath about her tainted masterpiece. I could already feel the pulling, washing, drying, greasing, combing, twisting, and complaining that was to come.

When I got home, the wrath took place as expected. Muttering complaints and curses, my mom detangled, washed, and styled my chlorinated twists back into their original state. The drummer came back with a new, kicking single pounding through my head. The scent of mint shampoo filled my nostrils, opening every pore of my scalp, stinging as it came close to my eyes.

My mother scratched at my scalp, unraveling the knots and kinks as I wailed in protest. She was not mad at me per se—just mad at the fact that she would spend the next few hours listening to my winces and screams for the nth time this month.

Sonia Kinyua

Barricaded in the basement, my mom turned on her favorite show to watch while she abused my crown: NCIS. She refused to put on programs that I liked because it distracted me, and she would be forced to jolt my head back and forth from the television. But I became fond of her show.

Magic transpired as my mother transformed my unruly locs. This was, in my opinion, the worst part—the part that made me want to go rogue and shave my head, freeing myself from my mother's claws.

Each swab of gel, each tug, each pull, each pop of the rubber band, and clatter of beads reminded me of how I would never have Rapunzel's long, golden locs. It was a reminder that even Tiana, a princess I should have resonated with, had smoother, longer hair that could be styled more elegantly than my coarse curls. It was a reminder that the thick, coarse kinks in my hair would always resist any straightening; a reminder that one water drop would cause hell to break loose on my hair in the form of fuzzy curls. It reminded me how I would never be able to just wake up, brush my hair, and go to school, a reminder that I would never swim without that skin-tight neon cap that traps even the brightest of ideas inside. It was a reminder that no matter how much I try, no matter how many flat irons pass through my curls, no matter how much I oppress my curls into a silk press, no matter how much I try to convince myself, I would never be like the girls in my class. I would never be like the girls at the pool or the beach. I would forever be the nappy-headed Black girl.

At the time, being Black was not beautiful; it was a burden the universe placed upon me. Despite my mother's mantra, society told me otherwise. Soon the small voice in my head would do everything to deny the Blackness I should have celebrated.

Braids became a safe space. Neat, parted, clean. They were reliable, straight, and didn't get tangled by an ounce of humidity. I could change the colors every month without damage, not having to style my hair every day.

Every other month, my mother and I commuted to the African braid shop. The sounds of Motherland tongues and television buzzed through the shop. *Expression 350* became my signature color. The ginger hair flowed down onto my back as the hairdresser slicked my edges into a tight braid. My mom always criticized the tightness of my hair, chanting how my hair was going to break off if I didn't give it a rest.

My aunt persuaded her into getting locs; then, a new, irritating mantra emerged about how liberating locs were. They both nagged about me getting dreads, *Sisterlocs*, or something other than the braids I loved. I simply ignored their unsolicited advice, still enjoying the bliss of my slicked straight braids. I almost felt beautiful.

***

The summer before high school is what made me hate my hair. With COVID, the trips to the shop ceased, and I was forced to wear my natural curls. I spent hours detangling, slicking, and hiding the curls and coils that would frizz in the hot Texas heat. Every strand was a symbol of self-loathing, a fear of an unfamiliar version of myself. I hid the curls, tucking them away in the comfort of invisibility. I once again became the girl in the swim cap, hiding from her classmates.

My sophomore year allowed me to create a new persona. I forced my hair back into braids, never outing its curly nature, damaging my roots. Then, my first state marching competition forced me to expose my curls. My color guard director complained about how my hair differed from everyone else's pristine, slick buns. So, I spent hours straightening with mounds of gel plastering my curls into the oppressive style.

After the exhausting performance, I released my hair from its anguish, expecting my curls to welcome me. However, when my once-tight rings remained straight, devastation hit. The straight pieces fell to the ground. I had always feared bringing shears through my curls, but those shears became my savior, protecting my rings from the damage done. And I continued pulling, tugging, burning, and hiding myself—my identity, my truth.

Sonia Kinyua

I told myself the various braid styles were symbols of expression, but I knew it was a facade. I feared my hair and feared myself.

In the spring of junior year, I experimented with a new mix of brown and blonde braids. The ringlets almost mimicked the curls I hid; the familiarity caused me to cling to the style. I never wanted to part with them. My mom told me she would interlock my hair so that my parts looked new. I didn't think much of it; I got to keep the golden braids longer. The interlocking continued, slowly revealing more of my natural hair each time.

Towards the end of my junior year, I was accepted into the New York Times Summer Academy. I wanted to celebrate the new journey with fresh braids. When my mom revealed that the interlocking she had done was permanent, I was terrified. But the natural locs on my head were finally free. Accepting my fate, I experimented with styles. *Hairstyles for short dreadlocks* became popular on my Pinterest search bar and soon enough, I fell in love with my hair. Not just the appearance, but what it meant. My locs were not just a hairstyle but a statement of non-violent non-conformity. A symbol of strength.

When I went to New York, my friends and classmates poured out compliments. I gained a newfound confidence in myself through my hair. My curls were growing faster and regaining its health, and *I* was growing along with them. The need to continue damaging and hiding my hair vanished. Though I first detested my natural curls, I discovered beauty in letting them breathe and be free.

I didn't realize it at first, but my hair had sent me upon a journey to myself. Every twist, every interlock, every curl I once fought against was a step toward unlearning shame and embarrassment and relearning pride. What once felt like a burden, slowly transformed into a blessing—a connection to the women who came before me, who wore their hair in defiance and dignity.

My locs tell a story of becoming. They speak of my mother's mantras, her hands braiding care into every part. They whisper of poolside isolation, of swim caps and shrinking curls, of straightening irons and silent battles. Finally, they speak of healing.

I still remember the sting of the mint shampoo and the snap of rubber bands, but I also remember the warmth of compliments, the joy of watching my locs bloom with health, pride in sharing my loc journey with others, the comfort of seeing my reflection and finally recognizing her.

"Black is beautiful," my mother once said. For the first time, I believe it. And, just like the locs upon my head, I became locked into myself.

Migration

The Restless Flight to Belong

A Town on a Lake

Albert Christer Singletary

Albert Christer Singletary

ndy always took a long time to fix my car, and I knew that this day in June would be no different. He was expensive, too, and never failed to find something more wrong with my car than what I had brought it in for. I would drop it off for a brake job, only to return a few hours later to have him explain that, while replacing my brakes, he had discovered I needed new C-joints too—whatever they were. Before asking for the go-ahead to do the additional job (since he could see that I was wavering), he would carefully explain how necessary C-joints were, that without them the axle might go, and that, though the C-joints themselves were not inexpensive, replacing them would be much less expensive than replacing the axle.

The necessity of the repair having been put to me this way, I, of course, would give the go-ahead for the job, not without suspecting he was taking advantage of my ignorance of cars. But I did not go to him because I trusted him. I went to him because he could always fit me in the day I called and because his shop was conveniently located in downtown Burlington: One could have a beer, take in a movie, go down to the Champlain lakefront, or whatever, while the necessary repairs were being made.

There was a cafe I liked going to whenever I was downtown. Going there reminded me of the years I had spent in Providence working in a cafe and being very happy doing so. Since the cafe's clientele was eclectic, I always felt a little more sophisticated going there, sipping my Russian tea, with jazz playing in the background and the paintings of local artists on the walls—this week figurative, the next week abstract.

If I was in a hurry, say on my way to work, I would pop in, grab a cup, and leave. But if I had time to kill, as I did on this particular day, I would order a pot of tea, find a table somewhere quieter in the back, and write or read. So, after dropping my car off at Andy's, I headed to the cafe, with my black leather book bag swung across my shoulder and within it some writing paper, a few pens, and some books. The cafe was no more than two blocks away, and, once there, I intended to spend the next three or four hours at work on a poem until Andy fixed my car.

When I arrived, I was happy to find at least half of the patrons sunning themselves in chairs out front. Sometimes, there were so many people inside that there were no empty tables. When this happened, I would have to go to some other place that I was not as fond of, but today I had my choice of seats. After ordering a pot of tea, I planted myself at a table in the very back, just off the corridor leading to the restrooms.

I took out the writing paper, the pens, and the books, and set them on the table. The writing paper and the pens were, of course, for the writing I intended to do; the books were for reading, just in case the writing went badly, or I grew tired. I always brought the books along, hoping I would not need them but glad they were there should the need arise, for reading was a kind of consolation to me. It made me feel that my time—which I hated to waste, being something of a Puritan at heart—was, nevertheless, well spent while I had been unable to use it for writing.

To get myself started, I jotted down:

> *as though a droplet in sunlight*
>
> *light sits upon the leaves,*
>
> *as though after a downpour,*
>
> *the sun shines upon the trees*
>
> *as though a spot a dryer's towel missed,*
>
> *light sits upon a trunk*
>
> *as though it had just been washed*
>
> *a red car shines.*

Albert Christer Singletary

These were the two parts of the poem I had figured out already. While at the cafe, I was hoping to flesh out a third part that, added to the first two, would make them something more; because as the poem stood, it seemed to me as incomplete as an outline that had an (a) and a (b) but no (c).

I began to write and did so steadily for about ten to fifteen minutes. In that time, I felt myself sinking further and further into the poem, the paper, the white tabletop, and becoming less and less conscious of the snatches of conversation and the clanking of porcelain about me.

I had yet to reach the other shore, that mythical place where the muse dwells, lying nymph-like upon beaches of sand; but I was upon the bridge and, as I crossed, could hear the music of the language coming from the other side. Then, it was as if that music had been coming from a needle suddenly snatched from a spinning record: Someone was standing too close. I looked up.

A young Black man whom I knew by face, but not by name, was staring down at me. We often exchanged greetings when passing on the streets. I would be walking along when I would spot his dark face ahead, conspicuous among the mostly white Burlington crowd, and he, I was certain, would see my dark face in the opposite direction. When we were within a few feet of one another, I or he would say, "Hey, Brother, how're you doing?" And before passing, each going his own way, he or I would reply, "Just fine—hanging in there."

There was one such time that we passed in the streets that I was quite fond of remembering. It occurred on a cold, snowy day that I was downtown running errands. I was walking north on one side of the street and he, south, on the other. Wearing gloves, boots, a knitted cap, and a goose-down ski jacket, he was as appropriately dressed as I for the weather, but, despite his efforts, he still looked visibly cold; and when he saw me walking on the other side of the street, and that I was as defenseless against the Burlington winters as was he, he shouted, "Cold, Brother—ain't it?"

"You've got that right," I shot back. Then, we both laughed aloud as we each went our own way, the cold, snowy streets ringing with our earthy cachinnations.

We laughed at ourselves that day because we had guessed the other was not from Burlington, and as such, we both were still trying to adjust to the weather of the place. Our guess that the other was not from Burlington was an easy one, for there were few young Black men who actually were. On the whole, the young Black men in town were from somewhere else and, broadly speaking, had come to Burlington for one of two reasons, though, to be sure, there were those of us who had come for both.

There were those who, wooed by the University of Vermont desperate to diversify its student body, had come for an education; and there were those who had come from places like New York, Boston, Providence, and New Haven, hoping to find a fresh start in Burlington, a picturesque New England college town on a lake.

I was pretty sure the young Black man staring down at me had come for the latter reason and had surmised I had come for the former; and it was our different reasons for being in Burlington that perhaps best explain why we waved to each other whenever we crossed paths but had never stopped to introduce ourselves.

It seemed that he had suddenly decided to do just that when I looked up and found him staring over me. Being quite comfortable with our habit of merely waving and each going our own way, I was not so sure that his approach now was such a good idea. This change in his behavior should have been a tip-off. It seems so obvious now that, with him, something had gone terribly wrong.

He began speaking loudly and rapidly about how he had been jumped by some young white men. I sat thinking, *in Burlington? No way.* He stared down into my face as he spoke but was not really looking at me. He looked at the three or four men—however many there had been—that had emerged from darkness and surrounded him.

He continued speaking, now about the hospital, his recovery, and how he had taken his offenders to court. Still, he was not really looking at me but into the faces of his offenders during the trial and afterward, when the verdict had been read and he had won. He finally looked at me for the first time, exclaiming with much bravado, "With the settlement, I am out of here." And he was still looking at me when he said, as though in explanation of his decision to leave, "The white folks here are crazy."

"The white folks here are crazy, the white folks here are crazy," he kept repeating with the emphasis of someone who thinks he's making a point, original and profound. He would lean in toward my face to say it, then lean back, nodding his chin silently as if to say "uhm, uhm," and he could not have looked any more serious than if he had been Noah warning a fellow tribesman, days before the Great Flood, that the world would end in three days.

But for all his earnestness, I did not feel that he believed whites here were insane. Rather, I felt he was only saying what he did (loud enough, mind you, for the patrons sitting nearby to overhear) because he was (and would be for some time) still hurting—and, out of an unconscious need, was now striking back.

I listened sympathetically, but at the same time, wished that he did not speak so loudly. If he kept this up, I thought, glancing quickly about, it could mean trouble for us both.

Perhaps he read my mind, for he soon grew quiet. Feeling a need to introduce myself after he had divulged so much, I stuck out my hand and said, "I'm Robeson."

"Darryl," he said, reaching out in kind. We shook hands but then fell silent: I, because I did not know what to say; and Darryl, perhaps because he did not know what to say either, or perhaps because, after telling his story, he was exhausted.

"So where are you from?" I asked, relying on the usual starters.

"Hartford," he said. "You?"

And before I could reply, "North Carolina," he was already adding, "Been here about four years."

"Me too," I said, providing him with another clue, along with the books and writing pads on my table, that I was, and had been, a student. He seemed not to care.

"I'm out of here now," he said. "White folks here are crazy..."

"Will you go back home?" I asked.

"Maybe," he said. But he did not look too sure. And I wondered whether he really would leave. If doing so meant going back to Hartford, then he probably would stay, for Hartford was no safer, perhaps even less so, than Burlington.

What Darryl said next was directed not to me, but to someone—a blur, passing by the table and at the edge of my field of vision—having emerged from the corridor in the back, from the restrooms.

"Where're you going?" he said, bringing the blur to a stop. Turning to look, I saw a young, slender, attractive white woman.

"Oh, there you are," she said to Darryl. "I thought you'd be waiting outside. Come on, let's go." She began walking towards the exit, confident Darryl would follow, and I realized at once that they knew one another and that Darryl had been merely passing time, telling me his tale, while she used the bathroom.

"Baby, can you hold up a minute," Darryl called after her to get her to stay. But when she, without breaking stride, half-turned and said, "I rather be outside where I can smoke," he capitulated.

He held up his palm and spread out his fingers like a coach signaling to his players from the sidelines how many minutes remained in the half. He looked at me and said, "Just give me five minutes—five minutes, Bruh—and I'll be right back." Slapping my palm, he hurried after her. I did not think that he would return, but waited, nonetheless.

I tried getting back into my poem but could not concentrate. I was too annoyed, too amused by Darryl, and my mind, too aglow with his tale.

Albert Christer Singletary

What struck me most was the irony of it all—*Black boy leaves dangerous, impoverished city for quiet New England town on a lake*, only to be thrashed by some local hooligans who probably disapproved of his choice of whom to date. It read over and over again like the headline of a tabloid newspaper in my head, blocking re-entry into my imagery of light and water. But I found that I could read and did that until it was time to head back to Andy's. And, of course, just as I had thought, Darryl never did show.

I was back at Andy's a few weeks later with another problem—this time the muffler… I did not run into Darryl again, nor did I, the rest of that summer when I was downtown, and I was down there plenty—at the cafes, bars, restaurants, and down at the shore in the evenings where I watched the sky turn from orange to red, purple, deep blue, and finally to black as the sun disappeared behind the Adirondacks at the New York side of the lake.

The change from day to night was like some timeless, recurring scene from the Garden of Eden. Most of the time, I was taken in—coaxed and soothed—by the illusion. But there were evenings when, as the sky's violets vanished with twilight and the first few stars emerged in a deepening, widening, darkening space, I would think of what happened to Darryl, reminding myself that the universe was not as benevolent as it appeared.

I was downtown Burlington that fall, too, and that's when I saw Darryl again, walking sans his companion on the opposite side of the leaf-strewn street. Whether he had made a go of it somewhere else and returned, or had never left, I had no idea. I started to cross to his side to find out but thought better of it. He had greeted me with his eyes but had given no indication that he wished to stop and talk. He waved though—and I back, as was our old habit—before going his own way; and I went mine, thinking that everything was all right with him, for things were as they used to be.

Written Resistance

(poetry collection)

Mos-X-Tee

ETERNAL RESISTANCE

Forever fighting.
Fighting forever.
Forever fighting.
The invisible opponent jabbing my pen from even writing.
Hooks and cuts from the upper room that travel to the pen,
giving me the strength to challenge this opponent of sin.
But why fight?
Why?
To what end does it serve to pick up this pen of hope?
Can't I stop?
Can't I decide not to write and settle for flight?
How do I continue to rise just to realize I'm stuck?
Is it wrong of me to feel this way?
Yes, it is doubt that you detect.
Because I forgot to mention the knee that has been on my neck.
But even if I quit, this fight of life will always
be in me I must admit.

And since He is still seated on his throne,

what then is this turmoil except a lie that started in Lucifer's home?

My fight is different from knives, guns, and aerial drones.

My response to violence can be found in Timothy's instruction

of how not to be silent.

See there is a standard as a Man of God,

to not fight with feelings and serve my enemies my lightning rod.

For I know who and what I am fighting.

So while it's foolish to some,

I'm going to continue to call upon Jesus' name

when hatred brandishes its gun.

See his name is Our shield of faith—not fear.

So with his helmet of Salvation, we stand tall and declare

God's people are here.

BLACK TEA

IF I told Rome that I saw Jesus today, would they believe?
If the image didn't appear in the agreed upon way,
what would Rome Say?
Would my Private Revelation be seen as a public desecration?
This everyday Jesus that I see don't have no red and white rays
or sacred hearts exposed to me.
This Jesus is a natural man who has ordinary days
and wears a red and white hoodie.
Can you see him?
He doesn't appear alone and only if asked is his divinity shone.
Could you believe it?
Who is with him is a people that look like me.
He even speaks to me and gives me a name to call him: TEA
The Eternal Accused.
Can you accept such a Jesus, who looks like your everyday thug?
Or am I just delusional, and from your ideology you won't budge?

The Racists' Prayer

Our Nigger who art our Creation.

Look everyone!

We finally found one, and he is great.

Oh, thank God in heaven for a nigger we could celebrate!

He dresses nice and his hair is at a comfortable length

that doesn't make us feel inferior about his strength.

Professional.

What profession you ask?

Well, Our Nigger of course!

Here to make us feel safe and stay in his place.

Oh, we pray that Our Nigger doesn't lose his way!

Could you imagine if he acted like them others?

Wouldn't that be a waste!

Stresses us out with all that talk of race.

We let it go, why can't they keep up pace?

Oh celebration, for the controlled nigger in creation.

Hail Our Nig and may no harm come his way.

And if it shall happen, we will just choose another nigger

and continue to replace, replace, replace.

042223 - Should I Quit?

What other reason could you offer to not say Hello back?
Other than when you see me, all you see is BLACK!!!
What is it about Black that produces your defense
as if I am going to attack?
And what is it exactly that you propose I am attacking?
What does my Black skin expose that to you shows
that one of us is lacking?
But I said Hello and you just stared, leaving me to wonder
why my Black ass was hired, Boss.

I Met Harriet Cole
at the Park this Weekend

(poetry collection)

Aanika Pfister

Aanika Pfister

I Met Harriet Cole at the Park this Weekend

After: I Saw Emmett Till This Week at the Grocery Store

On a Saturday, by chance, before work,

Pressing a free finger down on the water fountain,

I saw her reflection sparkle in the gush.

Morphed naturally, her eyes closed as she leaned to drink

Cool, clean water. Her purse was filled with pink

apples and chapstick, and money. And each round

bite was crisp and worth sharing. I said to her,

> *I wish we hadn't met. I wish you earth instead.*
>
> *Wish you silence, wish you soil, wish your soul gone*
>
> *elsewhere, Upward. And wish we, both of us,*
>
> *learned nothing of lead paint, of embalming techniques,*
>
> *of keeping*
>
> *wet specimen.*

But since we have

Since you're here. Bite hard into the fullness of fruit

And tell me again about that job you quit decades ago,

How you took your last wages in your fist and

walked the whole hidden path home.

Fading like sugar in a full, dark cup.

Now That You Are Home

For Sara

The land has changed since you last saw it.
A road curves along the path of the hills,
Long and grey like a flat snake, it paves its way up
And down the expanse of Africa, and connects everything.
An infrequent iron hum fazes little. Not even the inconsolable
Southern shrubs and trees, who have not stopped growing since
you left, their greenness, toppling over the land, thick as tears,
and now, Joyful cries heave out.
We have worried over your welcome.
Does it feel the same? How was the flight? The change?
To shed yourself of gray European feathers for the familiar burst
Of African Blue. The sun burned at the thrill of it. The night
Was long. But finally, it is morning. When you are rested,
Go to Gamtoos and wash your feet of dirt and roam.
Soothe the tall aches away after your long walk home.

Daily Living

(poetry collection)

Alayna Powell

Alayna Powell

There's something about a white lady cutting my hair

that feels like blasphemy

        something about her tone of voice when she says

             she wants to *experiment*

                   – my hair *has too much protein*

          so strong it could snap

                   – something ungodly

     about white fingers and nails scraping

at my scalp and the man across the aisle wearing an american flag

shirt that says *don't kneel* getting his hair buzzed

                   – something devilish

about that too. I want to cry out

when a different white man who is exactly the same sweeps my

     fallen curls into a heap and displays it

        like a trophy

before tossing it into the trash can.

     I want to snap—

collect myself from the trash can, kneel on the necks of white men

and american flags and the pale lady with beach waves who charged

me one hundred and twenty dollars just to be tamed.

when I leave

I wonder how they'll feel about encountering *that black girl*

with the big hair – a short-lived experiment of darkness

in a white space

I wonder if they'll be proud

of what they thought was grace

the only thing worse than disgust – the feeling I get

locked in the car with

on the way home.

Alayna Powell

Latasha Harlins
(in Two Parts)

I.   I don't have to imagine you as a child.
      You'll be fifteen forever.
      Dead
since the morning

you entered the corner store

looking for something sweet

to drink.

It was 1991

and you were thirsty.

That was your crime.

You were black, child.
      Worthless
despite the money you held.

When I say *worthless*
       I mean *less than a bottle of orange juice.*

I mean
    we want your body

on the ground, bullet

caressing the back of your head.

II.   Old women rise early and you're no exception.

     Bare feet beating on cool kitchen tile,
     an alarm that wakes the whole house.

     There are plenty of things that need done,
     but none more important than breakfast.

     So, you begin – working around yesterday's
     mess as if it doesn't exist,

     relishing those moments before the sun rises.
     At this hour, the day still seems so young,

     as if there will always be more time,
     or at least enough of it.

     You put biscuits in the oven, bacon on the stove.
     this is daily living; stamping down

     the same worn spots as yesterday,
     marking the wood soft wherever you choose to stand.

     You set the table for two,
     figure he'll be up soon and serve yourself.

     This is how I want to remember
     you—sipping orange juice gently from the bottle.

Alayna Powell

Milk & Butter Bread

Months and then years later,
after it's been beaten into nonexistence,

I'll be sure I've found
the meaning in my mother

getting cancer. It was God
twiddling her fingers,

playing hopscotch on the meat
of my mother's breast, half

skipping over chalk-pressed lines
cracked into the pavement.

In my story, God is the gatekeeper
of guilt. The bearer of blame,

as well. We've only ever known
anguish in this vast womb, spun

by her: meticulous fingers,
palm swaying. When I return home,

there is a cool cup of milk
& butter bread

waiting for me.

I can't begin to eat
without thinking of prayer.

But as I blink,
it becomes just a memory:

pressing a half-empty glass into
the table's soft linen, just hours

before

Alayna Powell

The Seed

(Written from the POV of Nancy, Nat Turner's mother)

Who carried you? Who felt you writhe?
Who kissed you tender, wrapped you warm in burlap cloth?
Who shared thy flesh? Gave thy body as nourishment?
Who bathed you in the likeness of the lord?
Who taught you to read
                the leaves for the lyrics of Heaven?
Who washed you in the river? Spread thick tallow on your tough
skin?
Who planted the seed of your desire? Tended fields
        while you wandered the woods?
Who was first
              to call you prophet?

The Land of the Free
and the Home of the Brave

Jamella Chesney

When I moved to America,

I didn't know that, when I gave my name,

(which means "beautiful" or "lovely"),

I could make people's tongues fall out and their throats convulse. I

didn't know that when I introduced myself,

I had to say the name of my country as well as the continent because it

was never bombed, nor is it a famous vacation spot. Apparently, I have

several nationalities, including global south and third world, and our

postcards show gaunt children living in

barren plains with mouths ajar and flies swarming.

What was most interesting was that, even before I opened my mouth, my

name was a color—a glass of Coca-Cola or a cup of coffee. Apparently,

it doesn't matter what my passport says, cattle must be branded so that

their farmers can identify them.

One summer day in June of 2018, while visiting Washington, D.C., I

stayed in the home of a coffee woman. She obliged me to visit the newly

opened museum of coffee people

that recognized *our history* and celebrated *our culture*.

But my grandparents never sat at the back of any bus,

nor have I ever straightened my hair for a job interview.

Of course, the people before me also came on ships,

but not all green things that grow from the soil are grass.

In fact, where I come from, coffee only sees itself as a beverage just like

milk, tea, or orange juice, all laid out on the same table.

In America, I can turn on the tap and not worry about it running dry. I

can even order food directly to my door, neatly packaged and steaming.

However, if I ordered a salad with to-mah-toes,

The Land of the Free and the Home of the Brave

it would come without, because those don't exist.

If only my grandmother could see me now,

standing in front of the landmarks on her TV screen.

Sometimes, dreams come true two generations later.

When I moved to America, I learned that some people are allergic to

coffee like that old man outside of Aldi in Lake Grove.

Apparently, the difference between a cage and an open field is a checked

box on a form, but even cattle know that an open field is just a really big

cage. I learned that farmers in America carry guns and wear uniforms.

Before, they used to carry whips. Here, the

difference between life and death is how much milk your coffee has.

Is this really *the land of the free and the home of the brave*?

Maybe the American dream will come when I close my eyes.

Earth's COCCYX

(poetry collection)

Eaton Jackson

Eaton Jackson

Earth's COCCYX

1

shifted
erupting among lava's flotsam   me
mud-crusted, hurting self

muddy hands, shaving off some of it, notwithstanding still, the
blackening of me to be
casting shadows from peeing searchlight

dirt that now soiled your manicured self, your eyes drop
down
as water washes away, cleaning
off diamond-ringed finger, lavender nails also
washing the last of the nasty dirt

                                      off

sediments gurgling around, finally self-velocity
selves down   through   out
of porcelain basin, this dirt
Me

this hue   this man, that
tuft of grass in between, that you wipe your feet on
wiping carefully, the decorative patterns
in the patent leather, the last bit of the hue   me   this earth

2

and it was night & day
interchanging identities, in
shadowed imagination at an
            axis
rotation on a potter's wheel, destiny taking shape, pages
also blackened, colored in
with the nightmares that live
within...

so black & me became one, each
burdened with the weight
of a dense color
washing at the stream, the
night's skin
load-bearing skin

3

as within the world of darkest hue
broken drawbridges
     dropping
                    crossers
 like busted hydraulics of cranes
scattered   wreckage, dream
debris down there
 in the
cul-de-sac of burdened skin
half-dead   barely alive, still impulsively picking
out shrapnel, squeezing bleeding flesh up in folds of torniquet, for
the metallic outcropping of particulates, to pick them
out, as the reels run with the rapidity of a film of vicissitudes

Eaton Jackson

4

runaway   lines are
long-legged, gazelle things
busting from the link of being chained in the dark, dank
          underground
lines, with broken off bits of cast iron   running from
that hurting spasm, of margins   alignments   rules

mud tracks, ankle deep quicksand, around boulders
under the brow of hills that block vision of escaping runs
as panting lines   from a recessed space, time
the jump   jumping on a sow rolling-by flatbed of thoughts

hopping
          off

5

at a bend in dirt road that rises to the bridge, arching lazily over
               river of stones
now   lines, a stallion's legs   hitting upon flatland of loamy earth
thunderous sound of dust bowl mushrooming
controlling the eel-like feel of a tight grip on a pen

6

towards widening horizons… lines
ink-soaked   tired, pushing secret door
lines enter
up a spiral staircase, unfolding itself
a lighthouse view of underground feelings, that
set tires alight, in conspiratorial wind that now takes over the
choreography: infant fires into abandoned wilds of youth
effect running away from the cause

assumptions breaking off   bolting
galloping away from their

                                        carriage.

Eaton Jackson

But We Are Running Away Again
Through The Swing Door

back into the dark, where from the darkest parts someone once saw
butterflies mushrooming in dispersed rays of light
the cross purposes of
chemistry & alchemy
us   them   people just wanting only to be people

in the rich tradition of mixing anecdotal into cacophony of truths
slurry like reacted ink across the page
eyes turn around
exiting through
imagination...

into a night's mute periphery, others easily frightened of the dark
peering search light, splintered rays bouncing off
the black muteness of
me & this skin   rather

falls right off black & I

mysteries impervious into which
shadows creep onto bridge over water
hooded personas lean over
object
gravitational force

splash!

into the liquid silence, voiceless watery echo sinks
also
further down
weighted to burdensome coat
down
never to be found

the river is still about this
remaining a river to fish on
to boat on
to picnic on
to be diverted into irrigation trenches
forced by its primal headwaters
agitating
still sinking further
down
into the dark
dump grounds of Emitt's limp bodies

Eaton Jackson

Closing The Bent Lid: Silos Of Toxic Waste

but it still drips
drips
making deeper watery
depths
slipping easily off the tongues, pass-
me-down generational epithets
considered out of harm's way, where chemical breakdown
ought to, but
choose not to
remaining a
coughing asphyxiation that regurgitates on another
apology

one, barely audible
crow-bared out, from between clenched teeth
sworn to again   like the last time
that this would   never again be repeated   your true feelings
about me

it floats around the room bursting as bubbles do
and you slide down the hatch
to escape when red-faced
flicks of a paint brush brightens up the ambiance of
country club five course meal
another apology for speaking your father's tongue
about this those people
another apology, whose pulling threads

bruised, compressed lips
the attached cord with the rest of your bile still stuck up in
underbrush
yanked at   your lips opening a little more droppings of things
like
penitence

over time apologies become afterthoughts scribbled on
easily dissolved paper
soaked by trained tear ducts
ink-stained   ink-fingers
broken
along perforated lines
to be re-written again
cleaning up
wiping at the rough sandy
tongue
at the splinters of epithets
folded as wipes
mess nicely hidden in the
folds.

Diamonds

After blood & mud is washed off, diamonds snuggles up to
become a flashing neon   'girl's best friend'
allegory about
waterspouts of genocide
that diamonds had all this time been about
peace talks
a stone's pointed tips of erasure

about people who are not really people living behind the mountains
tracing in oil slick sand invisible demarcations
diamond's denial, that it didn't bulldoze what was left of
indigenous folks
because these bush-people weren't supposed to be still sleeping
on roll-up beds on top kimberlites lands

so the program merely cut & paste   them
somewhere   else

because diamonds are war bounties
boy-soldiers with pieces of their remaining chopped-off hands
aiming scraps of AK rifles on the numb hurting
of metal shavings in their guts & in the guts of the other boys in
other
where villages aflame set other villages bright orange
diamonds did it, kneading molding
kneading molding slaves & their drivers in the same mud pits
diamond's pointed tips   drills & drills
until cracks crisscross across the face of the continent of the lions

appropriated slices shared internecine smoke rises, foreboding clouds
in the distant about diamonds cut & uncut
new peace makers, changing of same guards
same busted veins flowing into the red river

diamond was:
once a village of happy children
empty now   ash where streets were
diamond is gently fitted onto delicate, waiting fingers to
an
eternal love.

Eaton Jackson

Pointed To Hurt Someone To Hurt Self

the bones in our feelings were so pointed
they pierced right through, making ours
a play of tenderness
so we could never be coerced into a pliable dough
into
onto
anything without
splinters,

tear along the finger's cuticles within
the world of this identifiable skin
occasioning
broken drawbridges
dropping crossers

like fractured high rise cranes

scattered wreckage &
dream debris down
there

and within the world of my skin
craters to crawl out of dust to shake off...

a searing burn that
our faces, holds expressionless about it
fingertips of handshakes bruises at each other...

serious muscles fossilized into
serrated rocks
points that prick   if it
was possible to smile

against the fact, that my only act
if suspicious   if
if criminal, is
is running back down in the cul-de-sac
of my skin.

A Child of Dreams

norm mattox

Norm Mattox

A Child of Dreams

(after June Jordan)

I was born a promise
composed of dreams dreamt by generations of ancestors
spread far and wide from strands of DNA,
dreams streaming like many rivers filling oceans,
building waves, landing on all shores…
dreams blowing like many winds over land and sea,
eyes of countless hurricanes named after a multitude
of grandmothers.

I am the story
that was told by the griots of a hive of villages
that became a myth,
that remembered a new detail,
yeast added to the rising bread that fed
the hopes of unfulfilled imaginations.

I am the poem
scrolled by poets written in long hand, stories lost to
the ethers, found in the many voices recorded
in the memories of the ones that have become dust,
a pile of ashes, dashed asunder by steps
taken over hallowed grounds.

I am the last dream dreamt
you can barely remember,
details fading in fog you wake up to,
symbols you remember while people and places
disappear in the trying to remember.

A Child of Dreams

I am the memory of dreams flowing like a mudslide,
      a mishmash of flotsam and jetsam.

I am the story worth being told over, and over, and over again
      to children being put to sleep,
      not going to sleep.

I am the poem worth being written, memorized,
      spat into a microphone's ear,
      blurted out of speakers' mouths.

I am a promise worth keeping…

our mother's intention

i am the harvest
planted in fallow ground
my roots dig deep
sprawl in all directions

my seed planted
generations ago give birth to me
i germinate with a purpose
i hear air enter my body

mother earth meets me
where i am
sends me love messages
from beyond the veil

ancestors
on the wind
on a breeze
a hummingbird's whisper

Norm Mattox

water flows through my roots
the wisdom of my ancestors
nourishes
         evolution
                  experience
                           and concept
from humanity's past
guiding my first steps away from the womb

a still heart   resonates
rhythms of earth rumbles
dreams and hope
buried in my genes
animate my life
with ancient promises

we are composed of the same
         wind
                  water
                           earth
elements that connect all of us

living eternally
we embody the potentials
for balance and harmony
a challenge calibrating
         the chaos without
a silent dance partner
         the chaos within

Chuquin's Revenge

Willy Lizárraga

Willy Lizárraga

Una

The image is persistent, almost perverse in the way it insists on being the first: the night like an ancient, empty, and abandoned theater and my mother in her enormous bed, lying like a corpse, moving only her lips and her eyes, talking to me as if remembering yet at the same time prescribing a road to follow.

"Think big, Quique. What would you like to be?"

"I told you so many times. I don't know."

"But you have to know. We all have predilections. We all know what we like or don't like for our future."

"Well, last Monday they gave us a vocational test at school."

"And?"

"The results say that I'm supposed to be an architect or a coach, that I should look for a profession that mixes art and science."

"I'm sorry but I don't see the art or the science in being a coach."

"Actually, the test said that I should be a choreographer, but the teacher didn't know how to explain what choreographers do, and since he knows I'm good at tennis, he said it was something like being a coach."

"So, the teacher modified the results of the test just because he didn't know what a choreographer was?"

"I guess so."

"My God, with the amount of money we spend to send you to that school. The worst thing is that they don't give you any practical options."

"Architect is a practical option, isn't it?"

"Only in theory, Quique. In practical terms, the architects I know are merely drawing machines for the engineers who do the actual work."

"So, you say I should be an engineer?"

"Well, unless you want to become another Chuquín."

Dos

Officially, Chuquín was my tennis coach, but in reality, he was a lot more than that. Sort of a mentor, a guru, a surreal role model. As a joke, although more like an insult, my friends often called me "son of Chuquín." They made fun of him (and me for being his "disciple") because he was dark and wrinkled like a raisin and so skinny and tiny the wind could blow him away.

Chuquín was well aware of all the jokes people made at his expense, but he couldn't care less. And to make sure everybody understood he'd been "vaccinated against stupid jerks," as he liked to say, he'd walk the streets of Tacna prancing like a peacock, his chest leading the way, like a generalissimo inspecting his troops.

And it isn't that his peculiar way of compensating for his petite physique didn't seem funny to me, but I was never inclined to mock him. In fact, I thought it was admirable the way he ignored "those jealous fools," as he'd say. Even my mother, blonde daughter of a Black mother, fond of making fun of people with dark skin, yes, even she admired him. "Because with Chuquín you don't mess around," she'd say with a touch of irony but also respect, respect that might've had something to do with the strong bond between Chuquín and my father.

They both came from the same small city in the central sierras of Peru, and like true highland natives in voluntary exile on the southern coast, they considered helping each other in whatever way they could, a moral duty, which in practical terms meant that Chuquín received a minimum monthly salary from my father and, in return, he had me as his "favorite," eternal tennis student.

I should also say that Chuquín wasn't the only coach my father helped. "Helping the youth of today practice sports," as he'd say, was an avocation for him. He was a generous donor of sneakers, uniforms, trophies and equipment to all kinds of teams and sports activities. He was also probably the least athletic person in Tacna—allowing himself only one physical activity in his daily life, a half-a-block walk from our house to his store, a distance he covered with visible exertion and never-ending complaints.

Where did his love for sports come from? The only explanation I've come up with is that, as a cunning businessman, he'd figured out this was a cost-effective way of keeping himself and, by extension, his import/export business visible and engaged with the community at large. Or as he'd occasionally say with unassuming pride: "It sure beats paying for ads on the radio and TV." I'm not sure however this is a fully satisfying explanation for the roots of his sports advocacy. There are mysteries, I'm beginning to suspect, that simply refuse to be demystified.

As for my mother, sports in general and tennis in particular were mere means for social networking, so it gave her great pleasure to see me excel in a sport played mainly in fancy country clubs, because "that has to be just about the perfect hobby for a successful young man, dear. You have no idea how important it is to know the right people." And if she felt the need to buttress her practical reasons to compel me and my brother to stick to tennis and not switch to more popular and less exclusive sports, like soccer for example, she could always rely on the idealized memory of my grandfather.

"Talk about a true English gentleman, my God, and a tennis champion at fifteen. Yes, at fifteen, dear. Remember that."

Tres

Fortunately for my mother, Chuquín wasn't only a devoted tennis coach but also a true believer in England and Englishness. As he liked to repeat with the casual pomposity of a self-appointed ambassador of England to Peru, official emissary of "civilization" with a capital C, the living embodiment of what we, "barbarian" Peruvians, should try to emulate, "Only an incredibly sophisticated country could create a sport of such refined civility. Think about it, Quique. In tennis, there is no physical contact. So, no matter how ferocious the fight is, it never gets violent. Plus, in the end, you always get to shake hands."

One thing. No matter how strong and flexible the Anglo-Saxon/tennis connection between my mother and Chuquín was, there were also crucial differences, none more important than my mother's fondness for the U.S. As she'd say to her girlfriends over tea and butter cookies, "I think we all agree that the British Empire has been successfully replaced by the American, don't you think? Well, Americans are just more future-oriented, more practical. That's a tremendous advantage nowadays."

One more thing. My mother and Chuquín's coordinated master plan would've had none or very little impact on my life if I hadn't been hooked from a very young age to playing tennis and learning English with genuine passion—perhaps because both tennis and English helped me believe in the dream of a life away from my sleepy hometown as some sort of international tennis champ. In other words, unlike my brother, I never had any problem getting out of bed at six and facing the morning chill, the dampening fog, the empty city, and walking the ten blocks to Hotel Imperial's tennis court next to Chuquín who pushed his two-speed, Chinese bicycle as he lectured me about Wimbledon and Oxford as though he'd lived there, and when it wasn't Wimbledon or Oxford it had to be his favorite of all subjects: the art of winning.

"'Cause it's not about winning for the sake of winning, Quique. That's easy and pointless. The only thing that counts is winning with style. Like only the great players know how to do. Like your grandpa. What a pity he had to die so young."

"My mom is always talking to me about him, you know."

"Good for her. And for you. 'Cause now it's your turn to carry the torch. I mean, if not you, who?"

Note, my English grandfather had also been a talented painter, guitarist, singer and an irrepressible bohemian troubadour, traits my mother preferred not to talk about because, as she'd say, "The artist lifestyle, my dear, isn't really good for the family. Grandma Calixta suffered too much because of it."

Fittingly, I found my grandfather's artistic side even more fascinating than his tennis champ phase, and as soon as I could save enough money from my weekly allowance, I bought the cheapest acoustic guitar in town. Then, during my first year of high school, I upgraded to an electric guitar that was so old it sounded like a tortured puppy, but it didn't matter to me—to us, really, since my three best friends and I were determined to form a band "with a totally motherfucking original sound."

We called ourselves "The Motherfuckers." We played hardcore, clandestine, provocative, foulmouthed cumbia. We weren't popular but we didn't care. We were "artists beyond good or bad taste." My mother, of course, was more than aware of my "musical delirium," as she'd say to her girlfriends, but she never said anything negative about it to me. Given my "rebellious, contrarian disposition, just like your grandpa, my God," she knew it wouldn't be a good idea to tempt me to defy her. Besides, we had an unspoken yet very real agreement that we both honored with remarkable consistency.

As long as I didn't mention anything about the marijuana I religiously smoked every time I played with my fellow Motherfuckers, as long as I didn't share with her the lyrics of our songs, all originals, all written by me, *let's go fuck our brains out, ayayayay, let's go fuck our brains out, ayayayay,* as long as I didn't tell her anything about my weekly escapades to the cumbia parties on the outskirts of town where I found all the inspiration I needed for my songs. And now comes perhaps the most controversial part of our deal, as long as I never ever mention anything about Grandma Calixta's Blackness or Auntie Amelia's taste for women as romantic partners everything was fine, at least on the surface, between my mother and me.

We had so many other things to talk about anyway. Like my future, a subject that as I got closer to finishing high school became more urgent.

***

"What do you think of the idea of studying abroad, Quique, like in the U.S.? "The U.S.? Really?"

"Your father and I have been talking…"

My father snored away in his tiny bed, a humble canoe next to my mom's transatlantic cruise ship, a bed that reflected his true, inferior status as a man in a household ruled by two formidable women, my mother and Auntie Amelia.

"We've been thinking very hard about your future, Quique. And considering how disgusting things are in Peru, my God, we are about to declare war on Chile, not to mention that every day it looks like we are becoming more and more like Cuba…"

"But if we win the war, maybe things could get better, don't you think?"

"If we win the war? Think a little bit, please. Nobody wins in a war. Do you get it, dear? We are all victims, especially those of us who live at the border. I mean I wish we could all pack and leave, but your father and I are just too old for a change of this nature. Anyway, your father and I think the best thing we can do is send you to San Francisco. Remember my best friend Marta, Auntie Marta? Well, as you know, she's been living there for the past five years and can help you out getting settled. What do you think?"

Yes, what did I think? Better yet, what did the Motherfuckers think?

"Fucking unbelievable, dude. You're going to the paradise of sex and drugs. What else can you ask for?"

Their opinion was unanimous, and it was, for better or worse, the only opinion that mattered. The four of us, like the rest of the middle-class kids in Tacna, had been raised, after all, on a strict diet of American pop music and Hollywood movies, programmed from birth to leave our small town for the big city as soon as high school was over—if we stayed, we could study to be nurses or teachers, or not go to school at all and become businessmen or politicians. I suppose it didn't make much of a difference to trade Lima or Arequipa for San Francisco. Or as my mother would say, speaking with her suave, nocturnal, insomniac intonation: "Think about it, Quique, what better way of honoring your grandpa whose parents left England for South America in search of a better future! It's a pity that we don't know anything about them because grandpa was left an orphan so young. Anyway, sometimes the best thing we can do is just go far away to start anew."

Cuatro

Interestingly and rather twistedly, I left "a military, communist dystopia at the brink of war," mother's dixit, to arrive in a country going through, not one, but three very real wars: the war in Vietnam, the war in the streets against the war in Vietnam, and in the same streets and with equal asymmetrical violence, the struggle (officially never a war, let alone a civil war) for equal rights for Black Americans and people of color. And perhaps because I felt ridiculous as a refugee from an imaginary war, or perhaps because I thought this was my big chance to finally play a rebel with a cause, accompanied by so many others just like me, or perhaps because among my new friends and comrades it was expected of me to be proud (even in the most cliché way) of my African roots and my Native-South American features, or perhaps just because as an ex-punk, cumbia bum, I needed to be part of some sort of adrenaline-infused collective, who knows, but as I dived into the highly non-conformist cauldron of San Francisco in the early seventies, I noticed an alarming, radical change in me.

Without any effort, without meaning to, without fighting against it, I was becoming just another cantankerous, American kid trying to figure out what to do "in the richest and most fucked up country in the world," as everybody around me liked to say, elated to be the hero of my own

Hollywood movie and at the same time overwhelmed by the guilt of being the most despicable traitor to my family.

A traitor because I had quit engineering and school altogether. A traitor because I was totally in love and living with a Black political activist whom my mother could only hate because, yes, because she'd worked so hard, all her life, to be as white as possible. A traitor, and for some reason this one felt like the straw that broke the camel's back, because I was working (gladly, proudly, successfully) as a tennis coach, and I could already hear my mother telling her girlfriends during their weekly, tea-and-butter-cookies gatherings: "Oh dear Lord, I don't think I could feel more devastated. To think I sent my oldest son to the U.S. so he could just throw his life away.

"But as I told him, he's on his own now. I don't care if he's a coach, a taxi driver, a gigolo or a drug dealer. And I certainly don't care he's living with this Black, communist, atheist woman whose name I can't even pronounce because I choke. I just can't understand why he has to be so cruel to his own mother. Is this how he pays us for all we've done for him so he could have a life with more and better opportunities than he had here?"

And the worst part was that I understood perfectly well her pain and sense of profound despair. I understood what she was going through, in fact, better than I understood what was going on with me, maybe because I was just too busy finding my bearings in a new world and a sense of solace (despite everything) in not having to pretend, not anymore, to be an engineering student. And I'd say it was at this unique, pivotal moment in my personal saga that Auntie Amelia with the help of Grandpa Enrique (or Grandpa Enrique with the help of Auntie Amelia) came to me offering perhaps my only road to redemption, my only way to feel I still belonged to my family despite what I was doing with my life. And the way they came to my rescue, curiously enough, wasn't that different from the way my mother had come before (and continues to come to me) so that I'd never forget who I was and what I left behind when I moved from Tacna to San Francisco.

It was Auntie Amelia and Grandpa Enrique's turn, then. And instead of the intimate, nocturnal setting my mother favored, theirs was the sunniest, warmest, summer afternoon. The entire extended family, plus close friends, gathered around the big, special Sunday table now covered with dirty dishes, clouds of flies drawing abstract patterns above and between us. The steamed artichokes, the alphabet soup, the spaghetti with meatballs, the lemon-meringue pie, all carefully stored away inside our distended stomachs, stomachs that had been trained, like good Tacnanian stomachs, to expand without exploding. Also, the reason why we were all falling asleep as we waited for Auntie Amelia to begin telling us about "the ancient world," as we, the kids, called it. Or as my mother would say without pretense at disguising her jealousy at her older sister for being such a commanding storyteller, "I guess it's time to hear your goddamned Chilean occupation stories again, isn't it?"

Sure, it was. Besides, Auntie Amelia was born "a poet, not a poetess," as she always made clear, so we expected nothing less than a poetic feast, an experience that came as close as it could to listening to a mythical fabulist who, once she knew she had our undivided attention, would start her performance saying things like, "You know, some claim life is a mirage, an illusion; or a dream, as Calderón de la Barca believed. I'm afraid, though, they have no idea what they're talking about. For life, if anything, sorry Calderón, is theater. The purest form of it. And there's nothing more real than that."

Cinco

Let's say, assuming there is a benefit in hindsight, that now I understand perhaps a little better why it had to be Auntie Amelia, why only she, as a wise and canny, closet lesbian, an outcast from the "decent people's paradise," a phrase she loved to repeat, could embody the only kind of authority I could respect and listen to.

Let's also say that as an old-school poet who believed in "the futile yet real power of words," she was also the only member of my family with the right credentials to bring to life Grandpa Enrique in all his glory and infamy: "A hero who will never be included in the school textbooks. A radical, inflexible son-of-a-bitch who paid the highest price for doing something we can't even say out loud without blushing. Because one thing is to jump with your horse to your death to save your flag from the hands of the enemy, and another to shit, quite literally, on your enemy's flag. Because even heroism has a hierarchy, and what he did, well, yes, what he did doesn't qualify as heroic but quite the contrary, as a matter of fact, which is exactly, believe it or not, what he wanted. 'Cause he hated heroes with the same unquenchable passion that he hated flags.

"So, yes, let's call it a prank, a shitty joke, or an act of calculated provocation. Let's call it whatever we want to call it, but it really wasn't a joke because he knew too well, he was risking his life. But he just had this thing against authority, especially abusive authority. I mean he would've done the same with the Peruvian flag if he felt he had to. He was a true anarchist, I suppose. Although if you called him an anarchist, he'd punch you in the face. 'I am who I am, and I don't need anybody putting labels on me,' he'd say. Imagine living with a man like that. Ay, dear Lord, Mami Calixta had to be a saint. She's the one who deserves a monument, really…"

Auntie Amelia was on. We were at her mercy, and we were expected to be her audience and her chorus, responding, even questioning what she said, something Auntie Josefina, the middle sister, tall and humorless, all bones and edges, who sat next to Auntie Amelia, did rather well. "Well, I think that's not true, Amelita. As far as I can remember…"

It was Auntie Josefina now telling her version of the story, a version that might've been closer to the truth, but that we didn't care to listen to.

Willy Lizárraga

We weren't there to learn "the truth," anyway. We weren't there, in fact, to listen to anybody but Auntie Amelia, who took all the poetic license she needed to recreate something like the emotional fabric of my grandfather's "questionable, heroic/anti-heroic act of resistance." And fortunately for me (and the family theater), Uncle Roberto, big, round, dark, bald and smooth like a bowling ball, had no qualms about making Auntie Josefina keep her comments short and sweet. The same could be said of Helen, Omar and Hugo, my favorite cousins who taught me to dance the twist, the cha-cha and the merengue, and took me to the dance competitions at Radio Latina where one of them always won first prize.

Auntie Olga and Uncle Raul, who weren't really related to us but were practically family, also knew how to deal with Auntie Josefina's urges to correct her older sister. And their daughter, Lily, was even better than them: Lily who preferred to sit as far away from Hugo and Omar because they were too excited by her beauty and wouldn't leave her alone, the reason why she sat next to me, usually to my left. To my right sat Flavio, my father's right hand at his shop, his "adopted son," as my mother called him with enough irony in her delivery to suggest she was tired of him coming to eat lunch with us every day. And it wasn't that she had anything against feeding him well for as many days as he wanted. It was mainly because Flavio was fond of wearing "the cheapest, tackiest and loudest cologne, my God," as my mother would say, holding her nose.

Which reminds me: if the weather allowed, and most of the time it did, we had lunch al fresco, in the patio, the purple bougainvillea providing a spotted, refreshing shade and the breeze coming from the mountains whisking away Flavio's dense, in-your-face stench. Which also reminds me: although the Sunday table was an expandable and retractable stage, depending on the amount of family and friends we had over, we (and the expandable and retractable 'we') always sat at the same place in relation to each other. My brother Pocho, for instance, always had to sit next to my father, right across from me: my brother Pocho, who in my memory is always too young to truly be part of the family theater. I suppose I can blame my older-brotherly cruelty for condemning Pocho to an invisible childhood with total impunity.

Now, of all the members of the always-in-flux chorus, Omar and Hugo, aside from being the least in control of their hormones, were also the most active (almost hyper-active) participants. They were irrepressible in the creation of the essential call-and-response dynamic that Auntie Amelia encouraged, the reason why they were treated by her as if they occupied a "special place in my heart, oh my dear children," as she'd say.

We were all Auntie Amelia's children, though. When she told her tales we were instantly rendered innocent and pure in our suspension of disbelief, all gladly transformed and transported to "not so long ago, yet long enough to feel it was a radically different time, a brutal one, when what was forbidden or not was arbitrary and capricious by design, so you could never feel safe, and you constantly had to look over your shoulder, every move a potential trap. And when you feel trapped, you do crazy things."

"So, are you saying that Grandpa Enrique was kind of temporarily crazy when he did what he did, Auntie Amelia?"

"Temporarily crazy. I like that. Don't you, Auntie?"

Omar and Hugo, always in that order. Omar the oldest.

"Well, as you know, Grandpa was an artist. And 'all artists are a little insane,' he himself liked to say. He was also stubborn as a mule and crazy selfish. I mean he really didn't think of anybody else but himself. And he certainly didn't think of us, his family. My God, Mama Calixta was left a widow with three young daughters. I was fourteen and could help her, which I did, of course, but, Josefina, you were six. And you, Reginita, you were not even a year old. And we all had to pay for his sin. Goddammit, Mami Calixta was the widow, and we were the daughters of a crazy, Peruvian terrorist. Imagine how we were treated by the Chileans. No wonder the teachers at school punished me and hit me for no reason all the time."

"They hit you with a stick?"

"Or maybe with a whip?"

"They hit me with anything they had handy, oh Lord. And I wasn't the only one who got hit either. I mean, what did you expect when all the teachers were Chilean and all the students Peruvian. Besides, their goal, the reason they wanted us to go to school, was to turn us into Chileans. Isn't it funny? We were going to become Chileans whether we wanted to or not. The human folly has no limits. And think about Mami Calixta, who normally, just for being Black, was treated like a servant or a whore, and now she had to face life under Chilean rule as Enrique Reinoso's widow with a family to feed."

"So, she started a restaurant, right?"

"More like a hotel, wasn't it?"

"It was a pension. And to survive, we had to take in not only Peruvian but also Chilean clients. No wonder Mama Calixta always said that Papi Enrique was turning in his grave like the devil, although he never had a grave. How could he? They burned him alive. Well, they burned so many Tacnanians, especially the most rebellious, the ones who didn't put their head down, not to mention the crazy ones like Grandpa Enrique. *Ayayayay*, how do you like your grandpa for hamburgers tonight, kids?"

The laughter, then. Nervous, compulsive, hysterical. The laughter that saved us from the pain, the anger, the nausea, the indignity, the shame we all felt and that, thanks to Auntie Amelia, was made part of who we were as a family. Then, after the laughter, came this burning, uncomfortable silence, all of us avoiding looking at each other, our eyes turned inwards.

"And you think that it was worth it, Auntie?"

"Yes, was it, Auntie? To do what he did?"

"He obviously thought so. I mean why else would he do something like that. But he's dead and we are alive, and we're the ones who have to answer that question on our own. And it might just be that there is no answer. I remember, for instance, Mami Calixta telling me, maybe a month or so after his death, that she felt Papi had left her with one big question unanswered. She said that she'd asked him many, many times why he'd married her: a blonde man, son of English people, marrying a Black young woman, descendant of slaves who escaped the silver mines of Bolivia, anyway, that was a marriage you didn't see in those days. It was rare, to put it mildly. So, knowing how rebellious and edgy he was, she wanted to know if he'd married her because he truly loved her or just as an act of protest, a provocation against his adopted family, against society in general that in those days was even more prejudiced and racist than now. Yes, she'd asked him so many times, and he'd always refused to answer. And now Mami was telling me how strange it felt to know that she'd never know."

Seis

Last image. My mother and I once again together, her presence next to me stronger than ever, as if to remind me that Auntie Amelia's place in my life couldn't be compared to the primordial place she held as a mother.

We were at the airport in Lima. She held my arm. I had already checked my luggage. I'd been assigned seat 26A. I carried with me two tennis rackets and a shoulder bag containing a couple of cassettes we— The Motherfuckers—had recorded so I could be accompanied by my best friends in "Gringo-Paradise." I also had in my bag a diary, totally blank, that I thought I would start writing in San Francisco. Finally, inside a brown paper bag I carried a bunch of black-and white photographs of my family, including one of Auntie Amelia sitting at the head of the Sunday table.

Mother held me tight. I kissed her on the cheek. My father looked at us from a distance that already felt unbridgeable. Then Mother kissed me back and said, "Feel free to live fully, Quique. Do whatever you want or feel you need to do. But never do anything that will shame you or your family. That's all I ask."

Survivors of the Sea

(poetry collection)

Zenobia Anderson

Zenobia Anderson

I. Survivors of the Sea

A steady rhythm of mixed bloodlines,
a blurred story we struggle to define,
pulses on—
waking lands of the American West,
wide steps of elevated consciousness,
on towards
West Africa, land of hallowed emotions,
across salty tears of haunted oceans,
wandering, *wondering…*
Will we be shunned by a dry-eyed coastline
of our found sandy shores? Or will we be
pulled in
warmed in our homeland's sun tide embrace
of Her long-lost brothers and sisters?
Heart: stay strong
for our blood shed in soil has been willfully
forgotten, like abandoned
old gardens
polluted with prejudice and yet, still
flourishing, *in spite*. Blooming wildflowers
of opportunity
through grounds of the harshest realities.
We've a home, earned freedom with high taxes.
A modern
complexity of Black Americans'
rough contextual history, ancestry
reflecting features African Black enough, but then,
not to be regarded as African, at all–
or American,

but we are ***all***. Spoken with the voice of
a stolen ancestor, with relentless strength,
innocence reborn,
and beauty, forever enamored,
and both feet grounded, on both Western shores…

II. Ain't You Here, Lord?

Ain't you here, Lord?
The prayers of my folk been fillin' the Sunday air—
callin' for your sweet rain of mercy
and blessin's for our sisters and brethren.

Ain't you here, Lord?
My prayers been fillin' the Sunday air,
callin' for your sweet rain of mercy
and blessin's for our sisters and for our brethren!
And I got's to have your hand to hold,
'cuz my spirit's dry,
and I done lost my faith in all of them.

How come our roads be so long?
Dark and windin' with Grand Pine
conifers in blood soil'd earth,
and the pipes got lead in 'em…
How come our road be so long?
Redlin'd to cancer alley 85 miles
down the Mississippi,
dark and windin' with Loblolly Pine
conifers in

Zenobia Anderson

blood soil'd Earth,
and the pipes wit all dat lead in
'em…
The weight be on my heart for
leavin', but nah—
there be blood in my streets, my
streams be bubblin', there's poison in
our food,
and them homes? They been crum-
blin'!

And why they scared o' me, like I'm a
familiar hauntin' they kin,
like they daddies haunted mine?
Ridin' horseback under a sheet of
disguise,
lit crucifixes, our bodies hangin' like
bundles of strange fruit.
Why, why come they scared o' me?
As if I'm the familiar hauntin' they
kin,
Like they daddies haunted mine?
Ridin' horseback under a sheet of
disguise,
lit crucifixes, all while our bodies swing, hangin' like bundles of
strange fruit!
Yet the ones fillin' the prisons,
twistin' in metal bins of isolation is
me?
Polite protest only,' yes sir', 'no sir',

putin' hands where they can see 'um!
Cuz fear come loaded, and that danger be ripe.
Yet here we are, by and by, trying to
stay alive by being still and mute…

We all made in Your image, but they
mirror's lens must be inverted,
'cuz all the beauty in my blackness, I
can see so clearly,
how come they's is so broken?
 All of us in Your image, but they
mirror's lens got to be inverted,
'cuz all the beauty in my blackness, I
can clearly see,
so how come they's be broken?
They ain't know, and they fight so
they children won't know
what came before—
Kingdoms Kush, Mali and Benin,
bless'd with the strength o' thousans'
of men. Gold a'plenty, hope a'tril-
lion,
and songs sung, as if, the rays of
heav'n sunglaz'd them vocal chords
shinin' ray-beams from within.

Ain't you here, Lord? Your children
walk barefoot and thirsty in this here
West.
My fists be numb from fightin', my

throat be weak from cryin', and I'm
so very tired of always strugglin'.
Ain't you? Ain't you?
Ain't you here, Lord? How treach-
erous it be, barefoot and thirsty out
West.
My fists numb, my throat weak, and
I'm so tired of always strugglin'.
Colored of the earth 'cuz we been
here from the start,
emulation and mockery, both always
present yet somehow nev'r seen,
so we keep on doin' our best, excep-
tionally, fightin', marchin', movin',
lovin', restin', dancin', singin' and
soarin' free!

III. In Admiration of Blooms

Daydreaming with the Peony,
petals plucked
fuzzy feelings
fleeting glances
as I pick the fate of one of my romances—
never questioning
the final petal, *he loves me not.*

To have no worry
of the future,
on the winding path I pursue,

I take a deep breath
exhale a wish,
holding Dandelions to task,
for whether or not any of my dreams come true.

And the Rose's
formidable resilience,
beauty wrapped
in defensive sharpness
without the judgment of twisted
faces
who won't hesitate, to call the police,
while we sit in dread of the Lilies
held in death's left hand, as the right
hand knocks, marking the final hour.

IV. A Sonnet for the Black Woman

A Black woman denied her humanity.
She bleeds, then hears others cry, "what about me?"
Magic, but the human parts need seeing, but
dismissive ears miss the point completely.

The Black woman who cries when she is mad,
may her gorgeous bloom transcend all blindness,
may sunlit tended soil help her stand,
and her tears be kissed by lips of kindness.

Soft Black woman, within soft hair, soft skin,
convinced her differences are gifts inherited,

she will be seen with eyes that see her from within,
a beauty of her own affirmed narrative.

A Black woman of free will and free mind,
released from all that comparison binds.

V. The Divine Flight of the Adelphai

(Adelphai from the Greek translation for sisterhood)

She lit up and soared to the top of
the pickup truck's sky-blue-colored roof.

The Texas sun blazed 'round sunroof metal aluminum,
her skin, warming, quick through the holes of her blue denim.

But she feels no pain. Boone's Farm left; red party cup right.
She floats, a wild scatter cloud of Afro hair,

windblown pink mesh crop top with an apple green brazier,
the Blackbird beauty flies openly with her arms out wide.

Royal blue flames with white, crimson cream currents, golden bolts
ablaze with excitement for her bon-
fire hazing initiation.

But the Nine bound her up, up, up and
beat her with a paddle blend of hickory and oak.

She's faded: no longer ancestor-black-box-tough.
She buckles to each hit, spit and mockery.

As silent Big Sisters, lift their binoculars to birdwatch,
and then they leave the Blackbird
behind, blindfolded in the woods.

In the nest, resting on a high voltage power line
lies a shaking bird, hungry for the Greek letters of sisterhood.

Pollination

The Bloom of Seeds Sown

Strange Fruit

(poetry collection)

Hailey M. Young

Hailey M. Young

Strange Fruit / Basket Case

I remember when watermelon
was just a fruit
and nothing more sinister,
when the pineapple left me
with a bitter taste in my mouth,
tongue stinging, throat itching,
when an orange slice
got caught   in my throat,
and I felt it
coming up my nose,
leaving scents of citrus on my cilia.

I ripened until I was a blacker berry,
but the sweetness left me long ago,
started drinking grenadine   with ice
to water down the taste,
strawberry summers are darker red now,
the color of that deep cut
dripping
down my leg
like cherry juice.

The Watermelon Woman (1996)

I do not know you,
yet I feel you
dive into my veins
to find the deepest red.

We are the same,
like distant poppies
connected by
a wind-blown seed.
They consume me,
get high on my mortality.

Now they do the same
to you,
my brother in arms
you cry out, bleed out
covered only by a strip
of gauze.

I see the phantom limbs,
ghosts still living,
shell of a bomb,
shell of yourself.
Hold fast.
Weather the storm.

Collect the rain
in your palms,
satisfy your thirst.

Do what you must.

Just don't let them
take your last breath.

Hailey M. Young

on not being able to find the words

silence is a fall from heights
that I cannot survive
words catch on my sweater
pulling threads into spool

washing machine
hands churning the lips forward
I am a record, broken
from years of use

the needle sticking
on the consonant
and the body turns inward
begging words to leave tips of tongues

Evermore

My dearest,
I hope you are loved
the way you loved me

breathlessly, expeditiously
like a summer morning
just before the sun hits
zenith

carefully, hauntingly
immersed in the waters
of the Nile just long enough
for our fingertips
to warp

furiously, beautifully
like the velvet of a curtain
closing around a window
soaked in
moonlight

awkwardly, childishly

skipping over stones
at recess when
all we wanted was
to swing.

Hailey M. Young

in the wake

white lily petals stretch across the floor
singing songs of ships still moored
lost in time they fall asleep
with drumming hearts
that connective tissue
the metallic
ocean of blood

the door of no return
stops pumping
those bodies out
blood flow slows
to a stream, cutting off
the breath

captain goes ashore
crew lost
in brainwaves
leaving those
clandestine travelers
drowning in that dream
so when the wound
is found
they jump
they fly
beyond
the body

Ua La Mvua

Nick Bucciarelli

Nick Bucciarelli

i know the sun
najua jua
hides the moon
huficha mwezi
one time per month
mara moja kwa mwezi
so you can't blame me when they said *hamjambo nyote?*

but i heard

hamjambo nyota?

or how i cried when i learned *ua* means flower

ua means kill

mtoto asked,

do you have forests in your country? teach me, *mtoto*, to grow

fruits for their seeds

i feel *pole sana* for leaving

pole sana means very sorry

pole sana means field of dreams

On Fela

Ava Tiye Kinsey

Ava Tiye Kinsey

For Fela Anikulapo Kuti

When he doesn't have
A horn for soul to bleed through,
What should he use?

Conch shell, ram's horn, or
Cupped hands over purple lips?
When he doesn't have—

Blow his nose and make
The chord? Cough or hum or cry?
When they take his horn

And enclose him in the cell,
Xylophone ribcage they play
With nightsticks and boots.

He whimpers B flats.
Bloody teeth, now misshapen
Piano keys. He screams

Scats in shrill curses
And rubbing his swollen cheek.
Horn and soul now gone.

Ancestral Love and Light

(poetry collection)

Christopher Neal

Christopher Neal

Light Therapy

Black men don't smile in pictures,
Except the one that Jesus took.
There was the crackling sky, then the snapshot,
But the smiling stopped when the son dropped.
Then, it hailed ruby rain like the plague of Old.
A warm shower, unsolicited,
And cold Horror for its recipient.
Then, life rewound to the moment before.
Such profound ringing.
My ancestors' talking drums, transmitting silence
Through generations in my tympanic membrane.
My failure on display, like this cooling cadaver.
Message received.
Lesson reprieved.
Quite the quietus.

Bartering life for respect ain't no transaction at all.
And neither is trading permanent rest for temporary loss.
But this brick-and-mortar wilderness ain't the result of
The American Failure.
It's a testament to its efficacy.
You see, we come from land so 'live,
You felt its pulse in the soil,
To this belt so hot,
When you seep pain, it boils.
Yet, stranger fruits grow.

And so,
I heave and ho.
Grab my shovel to hearse this hurt.
Leave the body for the streets.
Just one mo' message to be relayed.
 I rehearse my lines,
Commit myself to the rebrand,
Teach Black Wealth and Black Power
Like I mean it,
And I do,
But I'm its antithesis too.

Beseeching Black Death in this Black hour,
Scythe tucked.
Killing kinfolk.
Living sinful.
Ain't no better than my preaching granddaddy,
Which means if living in the Light
Equals surrendering my Soul to their cell,
Then I choose nocturnal over diurnal.
I choose Hypocritical Hell.

Christopher Neal

An Abode for Sunflowers

It's the small things
That drive me crazy with care.
Press upon my emotional memory
Like flat irons on coiled crowns.
Warm like an elderly greeting,
Hey, Baby. Hey, Chile.
Thin as Black teacher patience,
Yet, just as cozy in its soft undertones.
You gon' learn what love is, boy.

That day,
You applied moonlight to your lips
And I thought of Rufus.
You hear Jimmy's Blues?
Bold and bellowing beneath like
Thunder in cupped hands.
Lips wrapped.
Rapt.
It must be showtime.

The Lord dimmed the lights low,
And we entered a montage of melody.
My main man Miles…
We inhaled heaven and all hell broke loose.
This is it.
The rapture.
It must be showtime.

Goddess, allow me to step up to the plate.
See, this platform ain't no thang.
Let me upstage this stage, hallelujah.
I see Orishas in this crowd.
So, let's sip.
And let mango courage morph
Sweet nothings into Everythangs.
Come on, Honey. Let's dip.
Trust me. It's go time.

Christopher Neal

'Round Midnight Blue

There's something bewitching about honesty.
Something brutal, yet genial.
Honesty is involuntary.
It forces both the wielder and the beneficiary
Below water,
Where the depths of the chasm reject both
Light and lies.
It was in this murk that I found You.
At a junction in life marred by the inane questioning of
Decisions long abandoned.

And me,
In my endless darkness,
My domestic dormancy,
Saw only the light surrounding You;
An aura commanding attention
At a time when only push notifications obtained it.
I should have known right then what You were.

One cannot see the Soul.
To do so would be an offense against
The Divine Mothers
And so we close our physical eyes and
Open the One bestowed at birth,
Our metaphysical measure.
It pointed me right to You.

Somewhere amid all this,
An *offering* was made
And we both accepted with alacrity.
Yes? Yes.
And yes, every time thereafter.

You have made me feel—really feel
The potential of this existence.
Everything is both ordinary and extraordinary.
Everything is You.
You have permeated the Deep Blue and
The seas sing cerulean
Fragmented by the Light of Love.

You are the message in the bottle.
Buoyant.
Floating.
Floating.
Floating.

Selling the World

(poetry collection)

Matthew E. Henry

Matthew E. Henry

Homegoing

(Inspired by an asen, the memorial altar of the Fon people,
Benin Republic—iron, brass, beads.)

the chord binds them. double looping
each wrist circling the fire. all
save one. he's falling from center—
backward out of the round. away
from the red coals, the roasting corn.

the others turn heads, faces—
fear, astonishment, acceptance.
the youngest is on her knees
pleading he regrasp, extending
her portion of tightly coiled strands.

his arms are raised, but not to her.
they do not flail. seem prepared—
waiting—to be borne away. his chin
is tilted upward. eyes clear as
the unfrayed end of his rope.

Bust of Akhenaten

(Inspired by "Bust of Akhenaten" by
Joseph Lindon Smith, 1908—oil on canvas.)

it's the blood smeared about your neck,
behind and in your ear. the cracks strangled
into marble—the rusty finger and palm prints
almost in evidence—extending up, bisecting
a royal headpiece dappled in copper.

who did this to you? the same pale hands
who compressed your lips and cheekbones,
thinned your nose? who drained
the milk chocolate from your face?

Matthew E. Henry

Quilt

*(Inspired by "As We Rise: Photography, the Black Atlantic Exhibit."
Peabody Essex Museum, December 2023.)*

beautiful pictures of Blackness uniquely captured—a Black eye
held to a Black lens. Black views often unseen by Them, by Us.
portraits of life as life. in response to nothing.
no ontological needing of *another*. no being *othered*. just being.
no oppression: no whips or chains or necks in nooses. no cops,
hooded or in naked faced blues. no poverty or crack cliches.
no running with purses or athletic balls. no jigaboos
or flagrant coonery. no *Stop the Violence* or Million Man
Marches. there is no need for Black fists raised in defiance
when Black lives actually matter, when "the luxury
of having nothing to prove" is assumed. it's simply all Black
everything in every shot. reclining with a tumbler of scotch
or appropriately sweetened Kool-Aid. cigars or cigarettes
dangling from full lips. couples in fur coats and nice cars.
others in Sunday best, Bible in hand. or simply holding each other
instead of generational trauma, or both at the same time, but not
the single story Their white lenses behold. fly fishing
and board game playing and TV watching and fighting
with siblings and B-boys stunting on stoops, street corners,
and subways. Black and beautiful in outfits that cringe and laugh and fly
and nostalgia us from the 60s, 70s, 80s, 90s, and now—
bell bottoms, booty shorts, suspenders, Hammer pants, bikini tops,
big-white-Ts, zoot suits. and the hair: bald heads and afros, twists
and braids, fades with knife-sharp parts, Jheri curls and perms,

natural nappy or with curlers still in. mid-wave brushing or sitting
on the kitchen floor before your momma, hoping the hot comb
don't hit your scalp, that pink lotion will soothe like head wraps
and fitted caps on a cold day. sometimes the smiles are forced,
but in a family way—a "do-it-for-your-grandmother"
or "the Gram" sort of way. arms crossed, eyes straight ahead,
but still the love is there. the swag is there. the cool, the hip,
the fresh to death. like the shots of us dancing how and when
we want regardless of who is watching. crisp and blurred ballroom
and roger-rabbit and running man and wop and dancehall and
ballet and tap and twerk and electric and cha-cha slide. it's simple
and everywhere Black. Lagos. Boston. Bodibe. Kingston. Accora.
Montego Bay. Jersey City. Podor. Decatur. Bamako. Asmara.
Belo Horizonte. Denver. dark and light skins—high-yellow,
chestnut, café au lait, milk chocolate, midnight—but always
appropriately lit, out of shade and shadows. f-stop and shutter
speed on point. always in focus. because it's a Black eye held to a
Black lens with Black hands to capture our own Blackness.

Matthew E. Henry

Adoration of the Magi

*(Inspired by "Adoration of the Magi" by Georges Trubert, 1480-90—
tempera colors, gold leaf, gold and silver paint and ink.)*

see the darkest of the three kings—the wise men
adoring the newly minted messiah. Bithisarea.
Balthassar. Baltazar. his name mispronounced
into simply the *Black magus*. robed in red, blue, and gold,
he fits in the least. the only one left outside
the stable's frame. the only one whose face is lifted
to the celestial radiation illuminating his rich umber.
one hand to his heart. the other wrapped in linen
around his offering: myrrh; the God-child will need
at His crucifixion and burial. perhaps this is why
Joseph's side-eye never leaves the only smiling face.
is why he keeps one hand near his wife and child,
the other on his staff—feeling he must protect them
from the machinations of this first magic negro.

The Moorish Chief

(Inspired by "Revelation, Chapter One" and "The Moorish Chief"
by Eduard Charlemont, 1878—oil on wood panel.)

I turned and saw One like the Son of Man. robed in clouds—
shrouded in white from head to heel—and girdled in scarlet,
the fringes of His crimson sash disturbing the ground.

His countenance shone as the sun in all Her strength. His aura
rumbled as many waters. His woolen head was white as snow.
His eyes, flames of fire. His feet, burnished brass shod in desert
sandals. His mouth, a thin sharp line—immutable, implacable.

I knew every eye would behold Him, including those who tried
to pierce Him and all His kindreds on the earth. they shall beg
and mourn beneath the scimitar held in His right hand, the dagger
slung across His waist.

I fell as if dead at His feet. He smiled and wished to cup a hand
around my cheek. wished to say fear not—*I am the first and the last,
the living and the dead, the Alpha and the Omega,* but He remained
silent, clutching His garment like the keys of hell and all death.

2Black

(poetry collection)

Kandle Jones

Kandle Jones

GREAT GRANDMA'S GHOST

She came back like she said she would.

Great grandma was not a typical ghost,

She was a kindred spirit guiding for good

Just when we needed her the most.

She saved a life by invading a dream

Until uncle was woke and went to search

How she did it from beyond a mystery,

Like a Bible story from church.

She insisted that he get the baby,

That she was very ill and could die,

Even though he thought it crazy,

He took action from his bedside.

Across town, baby was found,

A deaf mute she was, you see,

The hospital in town

took her straight to surgery.

The infant child's appendix burst,

And her sleeping family didn't know

What pain the babe must have hurt

That grandma's ghost came and told.

Now this story is true that I tell you,

But there is no fear on my face.

For this ghost was grandma, so true

Full of love, joy, and grace,

a ghost with lace.

KINGDOM COME

If I could ease your load
By letting you know
How much you give to others
Just by being a decent brother
I would try to tell you, though
No words can accurately paint
The majestic crown on your head
You inherited your title
As a king you can never be less
Than you are genetically blessed to be
Stand tall, be *all that*, and never lose your vision
You have a job to do
Only you can be who you are
You are a unique light
Even when your job, your life, has a dark side
Never forget for some you are
An example—even a sample
Of just how real men roll
Of how good God is to know
When you have a crown, cap, dreads or bald head
Royal skin kissed by the sun

Kandle Jones

QUILTING

It starts with a quivering lip
threads a touch from patches
to little swatches of fabric from
various phases, various places of us
the first shirt you gave me
off your very back
was gray with a cartoon face
the hat from your kinky head black
and I use a piece of that
the jeans that romanticized everything
on that patch you asked
me to be your destiny
and on this very cloth
relic of the day, we lost emotional innocence
the day we became familiar
it is peculiar, we made love, but never had sex
without emancipating clothing
we made love like a quilt
and it was my first strawberry passion.

TALKING TO FLOWERS

Chocolate lotus lips,

a planted peach tongue,

and ebony seeding eyes.

I am the garden you greet

with thick calloused thumbs

and warm loving palms.

How can I be so selfish

to deny you me? To deny me you?

I don't know about tomorrow.

Next five years—too much to ponder.

For I am like an autumn red leaf—

fallen.

How can I think with boiling blood burgundy

in air? And blue under there, like your underwear?

Yes, I am too old to be a fool

and too young to be used up.

A soul of a certain age

can still procreate, but butter melts faster.

I have my moments of foolery

and the clock is no bother for

color-my-moments with music, my muse.

Sip me like fresh squeezed orange juice

before I spoil due to the mahogany toil,

the reality of no Prince Charming

or no 3 acres, no mule for farming.

My generational wealth.

Kandle Jones

What did you say?

Repeat that raspberry phrase

for we all have a voice here.

No need to fear any colored ear.

Well yes, times have changed, and yet—they haven't.

Folk still divided and united by love.

LOVE… of flesh,

love of power,

love of idols,

and all kinds of healthy religious love,

mingling with the fanatics.

We all love someone, something, even if it is

love to hate or love to celebrate.

SO HURRY… plant your seeds in me

that I may grow like a lovely wise garden

before I am too old to remember how to bloom.

HOMELESS NOW, CAR-LESS SOON

Just because I had a job
doesn't mean I was gainfully employed
or could afford my college degrees—
or even to eat, to sleep.
So, working low-wage jobs, 2nd shift
was one way to look as if
I was head-above-water 'til I got too sick.
I, too, was homeless,
but for my car,
which they could not find to repossess.
Only because it was my last link to hope.
But this, too, would be a rope that would hang me.
I couldn't afford the car either—
nor gas, oil, parking—let alone insurance.
I found ways to bathe
at the gas station,
the laundromat.
Then, off to work smelling clean
with a sordid secrete.
I, too, slept with the deer at the park
where a sign said, Park *closed after dark.*
But I know God's rules didn't deny me
park or simple joys of moonlight.
Just because the economy tossed
my budget like a salad,
and I made a pallet
in the car. Homeless today.
Car-less soon,
but not forever
This too shall pass.

A POET TREE

Eye candy of literacy
Sit with me under the poet tree
It's colorful leaves with windy, wet dreams
Glowing, growing holy, wise, sandy seas
Raining sonnets, psalms, songs of gold
Beige yesterday, neon now, future silver soul
Of foreign, of home
Of saint, sinner, some other zone
This black leaf is Emily
So dark, smart, sharply bleak
The red leaf rouge and profound
As Alice Walker's words painting nouns
The blue leaf, a jazzy ballet
Of sonnets, haikus, John Lennon's *Yesterday*
The green leaf with promises of now
From music, the ears of poetry sound
Alex Haley, Dr. Seuss, ancient poets, and the new
Prophetic stars of heart and writer monsoon
Romantic rage, roulette of moon
All are priceless jewels, alone, or in unity
All behold gifts of God, heart, soul, poet tree.

I AM

I am that little light that shines
Within your heart, inside your mind
That rises, floats, despite dark dilemma
I keep you warm, despite white December
I am the start when some say end
That little spark of blue you begin
The make-a-way-out-of-neon-nothing
To pave, to raise the road to green dream
I am a yes when life says no
And you digest a positive soul
That cherry confess to be inclined
To walk by faith and not by sight
I am lavender love despite hate
And tender touch that makes a day
I am of peach peace in any place
Find me with ease when you pray
I'm the fuchsia flower, blooming your soul
I am purple power: I am hazel hope.

The Chemistry of Hyperpigmentation

Celeste Haehnel

Celeste Haehnel

I followed a woman along a train platform for no other reason than I could not stop looking at her back. She had a darker complexion than me and a black shirt that was open in the rear. Then, I saw it. If I hadn't been jostled by the crowd to get my bearings and intentions straight, I would have boarded the same train as her, not realizing what I had done until I was in Upminster.

It was hyperpigmentation, right there on her back—dark splotches. Ugly things, I suppose, but my repulsion at them was not what caused me to stare. It was the simple fact that it is very rare to see your own back in front of you. More specifically, I guess, it is rare for me. It dawned on me once I had boarded the correct train that this was not the first such incident where I acted in an almost inappropriate manner because I saw myself in someone else.

Two months prior, at a morning work meeting, I crouched down to pet a dog sitting at my feet. Next to me stood a dear friend, a Korean man, whose arm drew my gaze—a light, reddish blotch exposed on the back of it by his short sleeves. I considered this as I reached out my hand to touch him, immediately pulling back, shocked at my actions.

This moment happened so unintentionally, so unconsciously. I did not mean to stare at the Black woman on the train as she applied makeup, but I rarely see it in person. I looked away abashed when she looked up at me.

I remember sitting in my mother's room, my legs hanging over the foot of the bed, while I watched her in front of the vanity, applying makeup or doing her hair, so that, through osmosis, I could learn to apply these things to myself. I cannot though.

The first time I got to see what other Black breasts looked like, it was an old photo of Grace Jones. And it may sound strange, but that made her one of my secret heroes. Well, maybe "hero" is not the correct word. Maybe it is the aunt or sister or cousin or somebody who could tell me that my body was normal. I wanted the memory to be of vanity, but it was a memory of my distraught 14-year-old mind attempting to understand chemistry. A memory of my wonderful, rather zany mother who had 25 years of nursing under her belt, attempting to help me in my efforts. I am more comfortable with words and laughter and quips, and she does not understand that. If something is complicated, it is for greater minds than mine.

"Oh, it really is easy once you get it." She thought this a rather encouraging thing to say, but I did not believe her.

Color Blind and Hungry

(poetry collection)

Carlo Kim

Carlo Kim

Color Blind and Hungry

You sit at my table

break my bread between your hands
rub the oil I pumped into the creases
              of your arms
thread the linen I weaved through the
              eyes of your fingers
clothe yourself in the words I speak
deepen your soul in the music I've
       released, the poems I've
       wrought
run roughshod on our soldiers of men
       and God, and embroidered their
       graves in stolen gold
              (wept as a crocodile weeps)
you've whipped my grandfather
hanged his son
shot me
took my sister and (unspeakable things)

       —my mother
       she cries most nights
       no crystal stair with
       which to shatter her neck

hooked me up to an iron lung and sent

    smog down my throat

tarred and feathered the schoolgirl

put me in a helmet, pointed this

    way and that

threw me a gun and had me kill

    the Injun' (more innocent

    than a friar with a blanket)

made me brave mobs to vote in

    this cowardly land

then asked me to show literacy to prove

    I am a man.

You sit at my table

belching and wheezing and sweating

and vetting your neighbor while

lowering your hands into your pants

and now you ask me to hunker

to quiet

to let bygones be

and to eat.

Carlo Kim

Say His Name

Your life was the prone vessel in which America invested its hate.
It was the Israel of antisemitism.
It was the Cayman Islands of race.
It was the side-stepping recurrence of a devil who
has been roaming for centuries
and seeking a new body
to possess, to put forth messianically and color
crimson, tear asunder on the fulcrum of,
and abuse.

And your death was only yours
for eight minutes.

The mob ripped your body apart as your head fell from the pillory,
they pilfered the cross from your neck, the teeth from your mouth,
manhood from your throat as you howled "Momma!"
		from the asphalt, from the depths of
suffering hundreds of years in the making, yet all at once
evanescent, bespoke, and yours, and yours alone

—I remember the fires and the pride,
the turbulence of millions who came out with masks to baptize
the nation, to save their souls, raising banners with
		your name, your face,
donning masks adorned with phrases and Afro picks with fists.
Crowds and chants and bobbing heads called unto 300 years of
liberty, 140 of equality,
		and 60 yet of fraternité, fraternité—

>   the kind of race-consciousness wherein race is
>   forgotten, to solve is to suppress, and to better is to
>   reject the epigenetic throes and luminous whips
>   clacking against the backdrop of the sun
>   and the memories held waist-in, wherefore
>   victory is to be Never Ignorant Getting Goals
>   Accomplished
>   with a cute smile, or demure golden teeth,
>   wherefore the status quo's counterfactual is
>   evident in that

Even here, in the daylight, in the North, in the land of the free,
can a Black man be killed by four cops, his skin baking on the grill
of the hard ground as the grease of his dripping slobber flows over
the folds of his fat. A spring day, where the trout are abundant in
Lake Superior, and the heat begins to climb the bell curve in
                                                    Minneapolis.
A spring day, where the men are wearing black tank tops to
convenience stores, brushing shoulders with the black and the
white
and the white and the black and the yellow and the red.
A spring day, where, as it goes,
new life begins.

But ex nihilio nihil fit:
All it takes to proselytize Europe and recreate the world is to…
All it takes to raise the stars and stripes over Boston is to…
All it takes to put black bodies on the same bench as white is to…
All it takes to raze the third police precinct and enliven the ghosts
        of democracy's past is to…
  die.

Here I Am

(poetry collection)

Anesha Grant

Anesha Grant

Here I Am, Just Walking – A Mosaic

My shorty whose locs are an
unsolvable maze
Whose thoughts are a blizzard in
sunlight
Whose waist is a beacon for my left
hand
Whose waist is an apple or a
diamond or a pear depending on the
day's 'fit
Whose mouth is a feather oyster
birthing divine wisdoms
Whose teeth are contrast,
sharpening burnt-caramel skin
Whose tongue is a serpent,
shivering over snow-covered
pebbles
Whose tongue is venom and
antidote
The tongue of a beckoning siren
Whose tongue is a retractable knife
My ay-yo-ma whose eyelashes are
butterfly wings in crypsis
Whose eyebrows are disobedient
willow branches
My mamacita-ben-aqui whose
temples are bronzed hooks,
anticipating their crown,
With a fresh coat of shea butter

My ay-sweetee whose shoulders are
sedimentary deposits
Are collections of sun-hardened
clay
My baybee-muva whose wrists are
jack-in-the-box springs
Whose fingers are keys and locks
Whose fingers are doorways and
deadends
My ma-wassup with the armpits of
fried porgies and oxtails
And pork belly collard greens
That evoke memories of hamhocks
and chitlins
Whose arms are *taut palettes* for
coconut oil paintings
And a fusion of red junipers and the
Lesotho foothills
Whose legs are guitar strings,
setting basslines
In the mellifluous sway of Sunday
morning hymns
My gorgeous redbone whose calves
are seasoned with cayenne and
coriander
Whose feet are milk chocolate
shavings
Molasses-dipped and salt-coated by
the river's basin
My hi-yella broad whose neck is a
mahogany hull

Anesha Grant

Whose throat contains the Middle
Passage
And echoes with the psalms of
death's liberty
My li-skin-ded lovely whose breasts
are wild gardens
And manicured redgrape vineyards
And over-ripened avocados
My nubian queen whose breasts are
cupolas for absolution Whose belly
is a forgotten seashell,
humming the oceansong
Is a hilltop mudhouse
My sis-hey-sis with a spine of the
Drinking Gourd
With a back of Nile silt
And the spontaneous dimples of
fresh-laid tar
My sssweeeetnesss whose nape is
of peach cobbler
And of honeysuckle that sticks to
the fingers and lips and teeth
My thicc-mami-widduh-fatty, thighs
of parabolas
That are oscillating arcs
Unexplored in Euclid's ancient
expressions
Yet filled with infinitesimal calculus
My hey-ma-yo-ma-cumia whose
rump is both peanut brittle and
Reese's cups

Whose rump is the fire-softened
marshmallow before
the squeeze of the S'more
My bae with the sex of a praying
mantis
A supernova and a panda
With the sex of a seahorse and
unanswered texts
My y-fee with the sex of a succulent
My xcooz-me-miss with eyes full of
harbors
With eyes that are galaxies and
wellbottoms
With eyes of waning moons
With eyes full of storming skies that
trouble footing
My hey-yo-shawtay with eyes that
are kindling
ever-burning at the stake
My lemme-holla-reel-kwic with
eyes of weary wonder.

Anesha Grant

The Unknown That Dwells Within

Ask a BlackgirlmaybeWoman to be feral
and watch as griefrage, softhate, heavyhickory eyes
approach.
Don't you know how mountains would tremble
if I spoke with my true voice?
You don't fear the way the earth would rip apart
if I loved with more than my heart?
Do you crave the violent winds that come to shame
tornadoes if I exhale from full lungs?

This nation cannot reckon with a feral BlackWoman!
It ripped apart her body to prove her skin was thicker.
It ripped the children from her breasts 'cause it knew
her milk was sweeter.
It ripped the texture from her locks and the locs
from her head to make her crowns look weaker.

Ask a Blackdaughter, turned lover,
turned Mother to show passion wild
and watch as rigidhope, billowing
voice, heartflint approach.
Don't you know fires would
cascade and swallow the rivers from
the warmth of my full embrace?
Your souls would char from the
sparks lit by the full alignment of
my spine, head held higher
than your shivering fear could bear.
Your oceans will burn to enlighten
the orca, cephalopod,
and porpoise of my prominence.

This nation must now reckon with the wild BlackWoman alight
it scorched the land beneath her feet because her prosperity
made it bitter,
it scorched the bounty between her thighs because
her unconquerable bloodlines ran too deep,
it scorned the name she gave her children because
its tongue had grown so woolly with opprobrium.

Ask a BlackWomanNeverchild to be unencumbered
and watch as hardlove, alwaysliberatedspirit,
furtive smiles approach.
You should dream of the waves that will flood your shores
when I am free to moansinghowl
Your mouth should water at the thought of tasting
my hard-won sweat.
Your wells should thirst for the nourishing aquifers
of my menses flow.

You don't want this BlackWoman unmoored.
You can't bear the weight of her half of the horizon.
You abuse her, you shame her, you fetishize her,
you doubt her, you disown her,
you deny her
you deny her
you deny her
And, still
She sings her fear.
She feeds on her passion.
She knows her power.

Anesha Grant

The Point of View Assigned to Me.

This world was not made for me
it is made of me
My blood floods her dirt and salts her oceans
Don't wanna change her
She is who she must be

I want my mommy
I want my momma to know motherly love
      to have paperthin fingertips caress her face
      a honeywarm voice whisper in her ear
      the knowing melody that the world will be

      what it always has been, and

      she need not take it onto her shoulders

I look at the world
This fenced-off narrow space
it has not been kind
it cannot be my home, yet
it is made of me
My veins carve her continents and oxygenate her skies
Don't wanna change her

I wanna change my daddy

      to hear him scream love and murmur anger
      to circumnavigate the full Wheel and be
      consumed by each subtle taste
This world adds new flavors to emotions he's never endured

I look then at these silly walls oppression builds
                     fear fortifies
                     sunshine bleaches

Change is somewhere
between a fool's errand and a
captive in a
princely menagerie
She is who she must be

I look at my own body
And I see my own hands tremble
       Parkinson's or neuropathy
       I wanna change this sentence.
This body won't change for the better
This body has not been kind
This body cannot be a home
it is made of me
My blood is flooded with salt
My veins refuse to oxygenate

I look at my silly body
I look then at my empty walls
I look at my world
My seas are deserts, my skies are
corners
The world
was not
made for
me
The world will not change for me
it is made of me
I am who I must be

Anesha Grant

Mageirocophobia

I did as I would in the kitchen
pacing before the fires
as though the stove was giving birth
poured a strip of molasses
in the heat, it fell like wax quitting the wick
I do as I will in the apricot twilight
cold water soothes my stiffening hips
dilutes the briny dry rub into a broth
gifts the kitchen floor with anise
in the heat, it jumps like hot oil
I did as I would adrift at the table
golden yams and mustard
greens adorn fried turkey
wings
pleased with the roux,
distaste in the conversation
poured a glass of oh-seven
Viognier
in the heat, it fell thick along my throat
I said what I said recovering your
mother's crystal
from the walls
eyeing the cradled maturing
plantains
pacing before the embers
as though the stove had died in labor
in the heat, my tongue hardens at the loss
I do as I did
I say as I said
pleased with the roux,
the molasses warms over the pot
in the heat, it sweetens with your
leaving

A Trio
for the Diaspora
(poetry collection)

Paula Williamson

Paula Williamson

Ada

Wedged snugly
between sinewy thighs
fine-toothed comb
sections delicate curls
leave-in conditioner
curl creme mousse
I grip your
hair between my
fingers   over   under
add more   repeat
hands shaky for
a moment   blundering
out of practice
but muscles recall
hours spent perfecting
this skill on
brown-skinned silky—
haired baby dolls

I brace for
squirming   tears   but
we have a
cadence from late
at night   you
coiled in the
depths of my
womb your delicate
kicks constructed this
connection your siblings
fixate on your
curls   ubiquitous giggles
miniature feet hands
Hermanita   Hija   there
isn't much you
need from me
a grace seeing
that I am
already stretched slim
but this one
offering a precious
snapshot into your
legacy   the multitude
of melanated girls
that have sat
between sinewy thighs.

Paula Williamson

Casket Sharp.

Your 75th birthday
I took you to brunch.
At first, you seemed indifferent—
uninterested in celebrating another year.

But when we picked you up,
your makeup was fresh, expertly applied
hair curled lightly around your face.
After decades of resistance,
you had finally allowed the gray to come in,
resulting in luscious, healthy locks.
A new pantsuit—
you were pleased
to be pampered.

I snapped a selfie.
No smile from you—
our first   and last.
Your obituary, in fact,
because no one else had gotten
a good picture of you in a year.

Dear Mrs. Williamson

You were never a quitter.
Half a century of smoking cigarettes
stained your nails yellow,
weakened your lungs and heart,
left your voice hoarse, raspy.

I hear you in my dreams.

"Do I look like my motherfucking head screws on and off?"

"Girl, you know my nerves is bad."

Always quick to question my choices:
provide unsolicited archaic advice.

Our riveting political debates,
your selective memory
for things you would rather forget—
my queerness.
Your infuriating, often reckless tongue
         an inheritable trait
                  if you ask my wife.
Your decorative handwriting
on post-dated birthday checks
in cards that always arrived
at least three days late.   Calligraphy
from years of having your hand swatted

Paula Williamson

for the audacity of left-handedness.
        You made sure
no one could fault your penmanship.
            "Don't let them change you."
And I haven't—
not even when that them
        was you.

My Familiar

Raven S. Wilkerson

Raven S. Wilkerson

He and I sit on the couch. He has his headphones in, I read an oversized book. Since the day we met, he has tried to get me to switch to audiobooks. He wants me to multitask. He doesn't understand why I wouldn't optimize my time. He doesn't understand that I am in no rush. I like to hear my voice attached to the wild, demure, or uber intelligent women written on those pages. Although fictional, those women live within me.

Two glasses of wine sit on the coffee table. The one with lipstick stained on its rim is down to its last sip, the other not too far from the original pour. My legs rest on his lap while he rubs my feet. He would say I benefit from his love of audiobooks; I would be a fool to contest. I look up at him; this is where I want to be. We are silent with space between his heart and mine, but we breathe in sync. I want to keep this rhythm with him forever.

Earlier in the day we watched the news and with each segment my heart broke. *What has the world come to? How can people behave in this manner? What do we do to correct these problems?* He sat still, silent. I could not read his emotions. I am not sure I wanted to. We are all dying. We are all sad, all poor, and no one is going to save us. We have always been dying, and sad, and poor, and no one has come to save us. Yet, somehow, we have managed to love. Love is our savior. We live in a world that makes pure love feel unnatural.

I sink deeper and deeper into the book I am reading, lost in every word. I look up at him again while reading a passage about mature people making love. He glances at me and grins. He has no idea what I have gotten myself into. These mature people are on a plantation. They have skin that has been more than kissed by the sun. From the description, I could be her, and he could be him. These people are mature, not only because of age, but because of experience—from all they have seen, and all they have felt. Their lovemaking is described sensually, almost unworldly, full of passion.

I wonder if he and I have ever made love in this way. I wonder if he has ever released his frustrations during our most intimate moments. I know all he goes through, navigating the transgressions of the world and from the Man. I wonder, during the times I have allowed myself to be free, letting gravity bind his hips with mine, was I releasing deep sorrows? All this time, have I been releasing my loneliness, confusion, and fears? A part of me feels shame if I have, and a part of me feels I wouldn't be me if I didn't.

I think of our kisses between love strokes. Were they reminders that we were still there with each other? We have a history of being torn apart. Perhaps those kisses provided us with reassurance that no one had taken me from him, or him from me. I question if, during those times of lovemaking, our ancestors were speaking through us? How possible is it that they have been reminding us of our duties and our responsibilities all along—to keep our bloodline strong? We come from a strong bloodline. One that has developed skills for internal and external survival, connected to the earth, to women who bled on new moons and lured men on full ones. Let that sink in and embrace what it is like to be from a bloodline of men who sharpened spears and bowed heads before they departed for hunts.

Did he and I understand the depth of our love? It was once comparable to a cool drink of water or a bite of bread fulfilling hunger. A cool drink of water and a bite of bread, following the denial of one being a human being.

Now my mind goes to somewhere more present. My imagination has taken hold of me, leaving me to wonder—will we make love tonight? Will I allow myself to love this man fearlessly? Tonight, will I show him my many faces? Will I allow him to hear my many tones? I don't want to scare him away. He does not know what I have been thinking, as I have been peeking over at him after every few words. I think he will be accepting of how I will love him tonight. He will admire my unique beauty, and the way I will morph into many lovers during the act. He is a creative man; I don't doubt that he'll make art imitating my moans.

I believe we will awaken the souls of those before us—the souls who found refuge in dark spaces, gently lit by the moon. Our ancestors knew that with each touch they could have been sent to the gates of heaven. And if this took place, it would send a direct message to kindred lovers, messaging how loving one another, touching one another, could not be done without permission.

I am not sure he fully understands my connection to these texts. But I think that after he experiences me tonight, he'll spend the next morning attentively skimming through that oversized book.

The Authors

of the African Diaspora

Noelle Kristina Barnes
Grand Prize Winner
Burning or a Bullet

Noelle Kristina Barnes, winner of the 2024 African Diaspora Award, is a writer, marketing entrepreneur, public affairs specialist, film producer, and community organizer. Born and raised in the historically Black communities of Opa-Locka, Miami Gardens, and Brownsville, Florida—where she still resides—Noelle draws deep inspiration from her roots and the resilience of Black Florida women.

A graduate of NYU's Gallatin School for Individualized Study, she crafted an academic path centered on empowerment, cultural preservation, and the transformative power of storytelling. Her work is also shaped by New Thought philosophy and ageless wisdom traditions, which inform her creative and spiritual lens.

In addition to her literary work, Noelle has built a successful career in public affairs and media, advocating for underrepresented communities and producing projects that reflect social consciousness and cultural authenticity. Her storytelling reflects a life lived at the intersection of activism, artistry, and legacy.

Y Kendall
1st Runner Up
The Kito Story

Y Kendall is a Stanford-educated musicologist specializing in dance history who returned to student life after tenure to earn an MFA in Creative Nonfiction from Columbia University. Her work spans genres, including poetry, translation, and nonfiction, with publications in Alchemy: Journal of Translation, The Hunger Mountain Review, Bayou Review, and Columbia Journal. She's received fiction awards from Short on Words and Writer's Digest. Born and raised in Tennessee, Kendall now lives near Nashville, where she freelances as a flutist and writer while caregiving for elderly relatives.

Hailey M. Young
2nd Runner Up
Strange Fruit (Collection)

Hailey M. Young is a writer from Princeton, New Jersey, with a background in Literary Arts and Africana Studies from Brown University. She writes poetry, fiction, and occasionally plays. A 2024 Fulbright English Teaching Assistant in Botswana, Hailey blends creativity and cultural exploration in her work, drawing from global experiences and a passion for storytelling.

E. Doyle-Gillespie
3rd Runner Up
The Feminine Interpretation of the Massacre (Collection)

E. Doyle-Gillespie is a long-time Baltimore resident and active member of Hampden's creative community. He enjoys writing, reading, and lifelong learning. With a BA in History from George Washington University and a Master of Liberal Arts from Johns Hopkins, his work reflects a deep appreciation for storytelling, culture, and intellectual exploration.

Aanika Pfister: *I Met Harriet Cole (Collection)*

Aanika is a Chicago-based slam and written poet whose work explores marginalized stories, especially those of Black Americans. A Drake University alumna, she's been published in Contratiempo, commissioned by Illinois Humanities, and is currently researching overlooked Black women while applying to grad school—and wrangling her three cats.

Alayna Powell: *Daily Living (Collection)*

Alayna is a third-year MFA student at the University of Alabama. With a focus on poetry, short fiction, and archival studies, Alayna creates work often described as "haunted love poems," blending lyrical intimacy with a sense of the uncanny. Their creative practice is deeply informed by a commitment to memory, identity, and the emotional weight of language.

Albert Christer Singletary: *A Town on a Lake*

Albert "Chris" Singletary is an Air Force brat with southern roots and a writer shaped by global experience. He holds degrees from Brown University (B.A. in Afro-American Studies) and Washington University (M.S.W.). Though largely self-taught, he was mentored early on by poet Michael S. Harper. He currently resides in Mystic, Connecticut.

Andrés Amitai Wilson: *Fourteen Ways... (Collection)*

Andrés (aka Dr. Drés) is a poet, educator, and musician based in Boston, where he teaches English and instrumental music at the Roxbury Latin School. He holds a Ph.D. in Comparative Literature from UMass Amherst and degrees from Columbia University and Berklee College of Music. A published poet and versatile guitarist, Andrés balances art, scholarship, and family life with boundless creativity.

Anesha Grant: *Here I Am (Collection)*

Anesha is a college admissions advisor and independent education consultant whose creative passion lies in poetry. Her work explores love, femininity, Black womanhood, and Black American Christian values. A 2022 recipient of the San Francisco Foundation/Nomadic Press Literary Award in Poetry, Anesha continues to write with depth, purpose, and spiritual reflection.

Ava Tiye Kinsey: *On Fela*

Ava is a writer and arts administrator from Dallas, Texas, now living in New Jersey with her husband and son. She holds degrees in Africana Studies from Howard and Temple University and serves as Associate Editor of Poetry for A Gathering Together Journal. Ava Tiye's work explores the full spectrum of the human condition.

Blessing Odunyemi: *Ordinary Magic (Collection)*

Blessing is a British-born Nigerian poet, writer, and musician. With academic roots in Law and Social Justice, her creative work is inspired by Yoruba culture and the everyday presence of the supernatural. Her collection Ordinary Magic reflects this blend. Blessing continues to develop her voice in poetry and music production as she pursues a vibrant and purposeful creative life.

Carlo Kim: *Color Blind and Hungry (Collection)*

Carlo is a writer and undergraduate at Brown University whose journey into poetry began during the 2020 Los Angeles uprisings. Born and raised in the U.S., his work reflects a passion for activism, expression, and personal reflection. A devoted Lakers fan, runner, and radical thinker, Carlo writes across genres, using language as a tool for both resistance and discovery.

Celeste Haehnel: *The Chemistry of Hyperpigmentation*

Celeste is a graduate student pursuing dual degrees in history and library science. She works in libraries and archives, where she organizes and preserves the narratives of others. In her personal time, she turns to writing as a therapeutic practice, using it to process her experiences and explore the world around her. Writing offers her a reflective space to express herself.

Christian Curet: *The House on Bar St.... (Collection)*

Christian is a writer, educator, and father of three based in Bethlehem, Pennsylvania. A lifelong reader and English teacher of thirteen years, he is currently pursuing an MFA in Creative Writing at Wilkes University. His work, which often explores themes of masculinity, race, and social justice, has been featured at Black Lives Matter rallies and academic conferences.

Christopher Neal: *Ancestral Love... (Collection)*

Christopher is a poet, painter, and kindergarten teacher based in Shreveport, Louisiana. Originally from Mobile, Alabama, he began writing poetry in 2024, finding joy and purpose in exploring America's social landscape. A graduate of Dillard University, Christopher also enjoys acrylic painting, sketching, and reading. He is a devoted husband and father of two, and this marks his first publication.

Cianga: *allegiance (Collection)*

Cianga (cha-nga) is a Congolese artist based in California by way of South Africa. An MFA candidate and recipient of the Cave Canem + EcoTheo's Starshine & Clay Fellowship, Cianga creates interdisciplinary work that disrupts and decolonizes language. Their art—spanning writing, drawing, music, and performance—embraces Black creativity as both radical joy and critical protest.

Eaton Jackson: *Earth's COCCYX (Collection)*

Eaton Jackson is a Jamaican-born, naturalized American writer who has spent much of his adult life engaged in the craft of writing. Now in middle age, he remains a devoted student of language, constantly exploring its depth and power. His writing is a personal journey, reflecting a lifelong aspiration to shape meaningful words that speak to lived experience and quiet resilience.

Elaine Joy Edaya Degale: *Sunflower*

Elaine is a Black-Filipina writer and educator who divides her time between New York City and the Philippines. She teaches English composition at NYC community colleges and supports literacy and food programs in indigenous communities through OperationMerienda.org. A graduate of Teachers College, Columbia University and a Frances Perkins Scholar at Mount Holyoke College.

Elina Kumra: *Titan Arum*

Elina is a BIPOC writer, editor, and mental health advocate dedicated to promoting equity and accessibility in education. She is the founder and editor-in-chief of VelvetPoets and the nonprofit A Brush on Recovery, which supports opiate recovery through art and poetry. Elina's work spans poetry, fiction, and essay, and she is widely recognized for her literary accomplishments.

Jamella Chesney: *The Land of the Free*

Jamella is a Guyanese-born writer, environmentalist, and mentor whose work explores womanhood and West Indian identity. After living in six countries over the past decade, she has rekindled her passion for creative writing. Jamella holds an M.A. in Environment, Development, and Peace with a focus on Climate Change Policy, and a B.Sc. in Chemistry and Creative Writing from Stony Brook University.

Jamil Anuva: *Melanin Child*

Jamil is a Jamaican-born American writer whose work seeks to inspire dialogue, spark change, and promote self-expression. Poetry has been a therapeutic outlet throughout his life, helping him navigate identity and growth. Now, writing is his way of speaking up and standing out. A nature lover who enjoys chess, sketching, and dancing in the rain, Jamil encourages others to express themselves boldly through any creative medium.

Kandle Jones: *2Black Poetry (Collection)*

Kandle is an American poet who began writing poetry, stories, and music in childhood. She holds a B.S. in Criminal Justice from Gardner-Webb University and an A.S. in Paralegal Studies from Central Piedmont College. As an advocate for social causes, she has volunteered with organizations like the Red Cross and MADD.

Matthew E. Henry: *Selling the World (Collection)*

Matthew E. Henry (MEH) is a high school educator and poet whose work explores education, race, religion, and resistance. He is the author of multiple poetry collections and serves as editor-in-chief of The Weight Journal and associate editor at Rise Up Review. With an MFA, MA in theology, and PhD in education, MEH has a passion for challenging oppressive systems.

Michael Eshetu: *Her Teeth are White Like Ice*

Michael is a creative short story writer from Melbourne, Australia, specializing in slice-of-life fiction. A physiotherapist and part-time university lecturer, he draws inspiration from his Serbian and Ethiopian heritage, global travels, and love for sport. Influenced by Australian authors Paul Jennings and Tony Birch, he brings heart and nuance to everyday narratives.

Michelle Oxford: *The Dream Blocker*

Michelle is a Michigan-based author whose rhythmic, lyrical prose reflects her deep love for music. A former court reporter with international experience, she brings a global perspective to her fiction. Michelle's diverse background and keen ear for language shape her storytelling, weaving together cultures, voices, and vivid emotional landscapes that resonate with readers.

Monic Ductan: *Leaving Gillespie's Pointe*

Monic, born and raised in Georgia and now living in Tennessee, teaches at Tennessee Tech University. She is the author of Daughters of Muscadine, an award-winning story collection centered on working-class Black women in rural Georgia. Her work has appeared in Kweli, Oxford American, and Shenandoah. A recipient of a Tennessee Arts Commission grant, Monic is writing her first novel about police corruption in a small Southern town.

Monique Franz: *Babe in Arms (Collection)*

Monique is the founding editor of Kinsman Avenue Publishing, a nonprofit press dedicated to uplifting BIPOC and underrepresented voices. With an MFA in Creative Writing from Wilkes University, she has published over 177 global authors and edited numerous anthologies. Her work centers on restoring stories from cultures impacted by colonization.

Mos-X-Tee: *Written Resistance (Collection)*

Mos-X-Tee (Most Excellent Theophilus Luke 1:3) is a writer, educator, and proud Xavier University of Louisiana graduate. A lifelong learner, Theophilus explores faith through the lens of Black spiritual consciousness and the universal Church, shaped by AME, Baptist, and Roman Catholic traditions. His daily prayer is to release worldly attachments and reach for the Divine.

Mystery Post: *Mississippi Mudlark*

Mystery is a Non-Binary, BIPOC writer of sci-fi and fantasy born and raised in Utah. They hold a BA in English from Westminster University and an MFA from Vermont College of Fine Arts. Their work blends the uncanny and imaginative, including a fantasy novel-in-progress set in an Industrial Revolution world of ghostly lore. Mystery enjoys tabletop RPGs and binge-watching Criminal Minds in their downtime.

Najib Abbi: *Est. 1991 (Collection)*

Najib is a 21-year-old poet and recent Health Studies graduate from the University of Washington. Born in Minnesota and raised in Nairobi, he now lives in Washington state. Somali by heritage and one of six siblings, his writing is shaped by global experiences, family, and resilience. Najib finds joy in nature, soccer, and storytelling rooted in identity and place.

Nick Bucciarelli: *Ua La Mvua*

Nick, American poet, is an undergraduate at Northwestern University studying biology with a focus on human health. Outside the lab, they enjoy reading mystery novels, playing basketball, and making tea. Nick is currently co-authoring a book of poetry and chronicles with Henry Zhang and plans to pursue his studies in medical school after graduation.

Nicole Doyley: *War is Not Why I Carried You*

Nicole is a Brooklyn-raised writer, speaker, and podcast host with a long-standing commitment to racial equity. With a B.A. in English from Dartmouth and nearly 25 years in church ministry, she brings compassion and clarity to complex conversations on race. As Advocacy Director at Kinsman Quarterly and host of Let's Talk, Nicole draws from her biracial identity and family life to foster understanding across communities.

Norm Mattox: *A Child of Dreams*

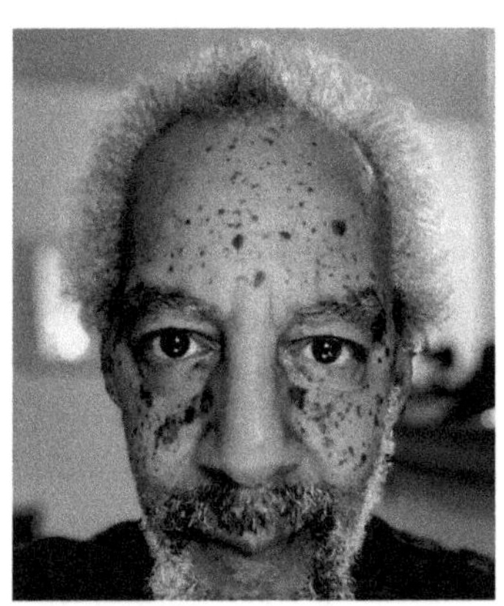

Norm is a retired Spanish bilingual educator from San Francisco Unified School District and a poet based in Queens, New York. His poetry reflects love, struggle, and resilience, with several published collections including Black Calculus and four crescents. A passionate storyteller, Norm continues to explore new forms of prose, deepening his creative journey through language and lived experience.

Paula Williamson: *A Trio for the Diaspora*

Paula is a Black Queer writer and mother of three based in the Bay Area. She is an MFA candidate in Playwriting at Antioch University and serves as the Creative Nonfiction Editor for Lunch Ticket. Her poetry and interviews have appeared in Manastash Literary Journal, Parenthesis Journal, The Chestnut Review, and Lunch Ticket, exploring identity, parenthood, and creative resilience.

Raven Wilkerson: *My Familiar*

Raven is a Bronx-born writer who found solace in music and poetry from a young age. Her work draws from real-life experiences—grief, joy, love, and hope—while embracing the intersectionality of her identity. Through poetry, Raven creates space for truth and imagination, using writing as both personal healing and a powerful act of resistance in a world that often denies her freedom.

Sonia Kinyua: *Locked*

Sonia is a freshman at Stony Brook University studying Political Science and Journalism. Passionate about creative writing and realistic fiction, her work is shaped by a deep interest in social justice and a desire to inspire young girls while exemplifying Black excellence. Outside the classroom, Sonia explores art, photography, music, and travel, drawing creative inspiration from the world around her.

Sufiya Abdur-Rahman: *Crossing*

Sufiya is the author of Heir to the Crescent Moon, winner of the Iowa Prize for Literary Nonfiction. Her work has appeared in Catapult, The Washington Post, NPR, and more, earning honors in Best American Essays. A VONA alum and Sustainable Arts Foundation fellow, she is Creative Nonfiction Editor at Cherry Tree and teaches college-level nonfiction. Sufiya lives in Annapolis, Maryland, with her family.

Willy Lizárraga: *Chuquín's Revenge*

Willy is a writer and photographer born in the southernmost city of Peru and raised in San Francisco. His creative work bridges languages and borders, shaped by a deep connection to Spanish, English, Portuguese, and visual storytelling. Willy explores themes of identity, loss, and belonging, drawing inspiration from the spaces between cultures—where the stories he cares most about tend to live.

Zenobia Anderson: *Survivors of the Sea (Collection)*

Dr. Aiyana Zenobia Anderson is a writer and dental professional with roots in Barbados and the Carolinas, now living in San Antonio, Texas. A lifelong lover of literature, she draws inspiration from voices like Poe and Toni Morrison. After years of private writing, she began sharing her work publicly in 2023. Aiyana balances her creative journey with family life and co-owning a dental practice with her best friend.